Curvy Nanny for the Nerd

A Billionaire Single Dad Romance

Piper Sullivan

Enjoy Spicy Romances?

Download Safeguarded for FREE Now!

Chapter 1

Brady

Nothing is working the way I wanted it to. Not today.

Not yesterday. Not any day for the past year or more. I can't concentrate. I can't focus, not for hours on end the way I'm used to while working. My relentless focus was why the first game in this series, *Shooter Alpha ONE*, was such a success, and it's why the last three game series my company released over the past four years were equally successful.

My company, *Winsome, Lose Some,* has been my wife, my children, my whole entire life since I started it at the ripe old age of twenty-three. I have lived and breathed this company from the very beginning, putting my heart and soul into every game, every app and every line on every spreadsheet.

But now? It's all gone to hell. I can't seem to string together enough time to make *Shooter Alpha TWO* even better than the first game, but I have to. I need to keep the momentum going because it's not enough to be among the top three gaming companies in the industry, and it's not enough to be billionaire before thirty.

I want to be *the* best.

I need to be the absolute best.

A loud shrieking noise sounded in the distance and I tried to ignore it and get back to the task at hand, tweaking the dialogue so it sounded more authentic. The research I'd done online and in person had given me everything I needed to improve it. Everything except time.

The commotion grew louder and I got up from my desk, knowing that I wasn't going to be able to get anything done until I stopped that infernal racket. I stood with a grunt and raked a hand through thick brown hair I hadn't done more than finger comb in too many days to count, steadying my nerves before I made my way out of my office in the back of the mansion and down a long hall that wound through the large living room and ended at the kitchen. Here the noise was so loud I couldn't hear myself think.

"What in the hell is that?"

Silver blue eyes that were identical to my own glared at me as if I was the cause of the offending sound. "It's the smoke detector," my niece Layla shouted at me. "I can't reach it. Obviously."

I ignored her rude tone and jumped on the counter to stop the smoke detector from making my eardrums bleed. "Better." I jumped down and stared at my niece through a plume of quickly fading dark smoke. "What in the hell were you thinking?"

Layla folded her arms, flicking the blond hair she'd inherited from her dad off her shoulders, and rolled her eyes with all the sass of a seven year old going on sixteen. "I was thinking that I'm hungry and since there are no responsible adults in this house, it was up to me to feed myself." She was being dramatic.

"You're being dramatic," I told her and glanced down at my watch to prove my point, but my eyes widened. "Four-thirty? It's four-thirty, why didn't you say anything?"

She shrugged, but the look of disappointment in her eyes made me feel like I was failing at everything. "I assumed you forgot about me. Again."

My shoulders sank at her words, spoken so frankly and simply as if she just accepted it. "I'm sorry, Layla. I'm working really hard on this game and I lost track of time."

"Yeah, yeah," she said with a dismissive wave of her hand. "You're busy and important. I'm aware." She held up her hands. "I got it. You don't need to worry about me." Without another word she reached for the blackened grilled cheese and a butter knife, angrily scraping off the burnt layer.

I reached for the knife and she yanked it away, tossing it angrily into the sink and the sandwich in the trash. "Let me help."

"I'm fine," she yelled and stomped out of the room. She didn't run, which somehow made it worse. Her controlled pace combined with her straight spine and squared small shoulders was proof that I was failing more as a parent than as a game developer.

I felt helpless, so I did what I always did, I went back to my office and buried myself in work. My sister was probably turning over in her grave at all the ways I was failing her little girl. Why in the hell did Marnie leave her kid with me, anyway? I was the awkward brother. The introvert who spent more time on his computer than with live human beings. Why had she, in her infinite wisdom, decided that I would be a good choice in the event of her untimely death?

Because it's been me and you since the beginning of time, she'd written in a note given to me by her and her husband's estate attorney, and she was right. Our parents died early and Marnie had stepped up to get her awkward brother to college before she made her own dreams come true.

"Dammit!" Now I was distracted by thoughts of my sister and how she'd come through for me every single time I needed her. But this one thing she tasked me with—caring for Layla—I couldn't do it right to save my life.

I wasn't good with people, not even small people. Hell, I wasn't good with seven year olds even when I was one, and now? Everything I said was wrong.

Until now.

Layla was hungry and so was I, which meant this was the one thing in this moment I could do something to fix. I grabbed my phone and ordered food, enough for lunch and dinner for two hungry people, casting one last disappointed look at all the unfinished tasks on the list beside my keyboard.

Later. I'll get back to this later, and I'll be more productive on a full stomach and without guilt weighing me down.

"Layla!" I called out from the other side of her bedroom door. The one thing I remembered about girls was that they liked their privacy and I respected that. "Hey Layla, can I come in?"

"Yeah, come in Uncle Brady." Even her tone was petulant, but I told myself it was what I deserved.

"Hey." I raised an awkward hand and smiled. "I'm sorry about lunch, honestly. I didn't forget about you, it's just that I often forget to eat myself. But now that you're here I should do better. I *will* do better."

"Just buy some food I can make myself," she muttered under her breath.

"I did even better," I smiled proudly. "Lunch is here. And dinner. Sandwiches and fries, chips, salad and even a few slices of cake. Chocolate and lemon."

Her blue eyes perked up, reminding me so much of my sister my heart squeezed. "Chocolate and lemon are my favorite."

For the first time since I became her guardian, she looked like a happy little girl. "I know. Your mom's too. She would smash them together and eat them like that. It was disgusting."

Layla giggled. "That's what my dad would say."

"Care to join me for lunch?"

Disbelief shone in her eyes, but Layla nodded and followed me downstairs and into the kitchen. She piled two different types of sandwiches on top of a mountain of fries and sat down. She ate without a word and that feeling of failure returned.

"Layla, I'm going to try to do better," I promised.

She sighed heavily. "It's fine, Uncle Brady. I know you didn't sign up for this, but you're all I've got. I'll stay out of your way and you'll make sure there's food in the house I can eat. We'll be fine."

"Yeah," I agreed. "We will be. But to be honest, I expected to have my days free to work while you were at school."

She rolled her eyes. "I don't like bullies."

"No one does and I get that, which is why I need to do better. And I will."

She shook her head and sat back with a sigh that held the weight of the world in it, her eyes darting around the table. "I'll be just fine," she whispered, taking her cake and the rest of the food upstairs without a backwards glance.

"Damn!" I needed to figure something out. Sure, Layla was self-sufficient, but she was also just seven years old and I'd left too much in her young hands since she moved in with me.

A babysitter. She needed a babysitter, someone who could watch over her while I finished *Alpha Shooter TWO*.

Now, can you order a babysitter online?

Chapter 2

Toni

"A refill, madam?"

The Maitre'd smiled at me as if he knew that the only way I would survive two hours of torture—also known as dinner with my parents—was with more wine.

"Absolutely. All the way to the top, Luc." I held out my red wine glass and nodded until I was satisfied that the glass was full enough. "Thank you very much." I raised the glass in his direction, smiled and took a big sip. "Delicious."

My mother was a stickler for decorum, as such, she has never passed up an opportunity to let me know how much I disappoint her. "Was that truly necessary, Antonia?"

"Truly? Not at all. But he offered, and I wanted more wine. What is the problem?" We'd barely sat down ten minutes and already she's found at least four things to criticize me about.

"You're looking good, sweetheart." My dad was the nice one in the Stafford family. He always had a kind word for me and found happiness when his only child was happy.

"Thank you, Daddy. You look like you've been making time for tennis." His skin had a golden glow, his blond hair was sun bleached and he looked about ten pounds slimmer. Not bad for a guy in his late fifties.

"Good, yes," my mother sniffed with disapproval. "But you've put on a few pounds, haven't you?"

Five things to criticize. "I'm the same size I've always been," I told her as I rolled my eyes. I've always had a few too many curves for my mother's liking, and by a few too many I mean too many, period. She didn't appreciate my D-cups or my wide hips, even though they were separated by a small waist that gave me the perfect hourglass, if you're into that kind of thing.

"Yes well, you've always needed to lose a few pounds."

Six things. "I'm fine the way I am, thanks for your concern, Mother."

She gave me that heavy sigh, the one that reminded me I was a constant disappointment. "If you don't slim down you will never find a suitable husband, Antonia."

"It's Toni, and I'm not looking for a husband, suitable or otherwise." She would never understand that while I was grateful for the life my folks provided for me, it wasn't a path I wanted to follow.

"A man wants a fit woman. Think of how much weight you'll put on after a few children."

I rolled my eyes. "Who says I want children?" I loved kids, of course I did, otherwise I wouldn't have become a nanny. But other people's kids were great because you got to leave them at the end of the day. Come home to more kids plus my nanny duties? No thanks. "And I am fit, Mother. I get plenty of exercise, and if a man doesn't like me the way I am, fuck him."

Dad grinned. "That's right, honey."

Mom gasped. "With that kind of language you won't have to worry about finding a suitable man."

"Good." I took a few more healthy sips in an effort to hold my tongue before I said something to my mom that I couldn't take back.

"Trevor Halsey is back in town after finishing law school. Suzanne said he's ready to find a wife."

"Good for him. I hope he finds what he's looking for." I didn't bother to remind her that I didn't know Trevor and had no interest in any of her friends' sons.

"Antonia, you cannot be a nanny forever. That's sad, and worse, it's pathetic."

"It's an honest career, Mother."

"Yes, it is," she agreed with a glint in her eyes. "For women who have no choice, who don't have the options you do."

"I love my job and if you can't respect that, then I guess you don't respect me. Still." I stood just as our food arrived and finished off my wine. "It was so good to see you, Daddy. Mother," I growled and walked out of the fancy restaurant filled with Houston's elite with my head held high.

By the time I made it the few blocks to the parking garage, because I refused to pay for valet, my mother had called at least a dozen times. I smiled to myself thinking how furious she probably was that I kept sending her to voicemail. I drove home, ignoring three more calls, and parked my car before I made my way to my favorite watering hole just two blocks from my condo.

I called Lucy first because she was my closest friend. "Toni, I thought you were having dinner with your parents?"

"I was, and now I'm not. You free for a drink or ten?"

But she sighed, and I knew it was a no go. "Not tonight, Toni. Lena isn't feeling well and my boobs are sore. Sorry."

New motherhood was harder than it looked. "Don't be. Talk soon."

"Are you all right?"

No. "Absolutely. Go relax while you can. Later."

I stared at my contacts and knew I would get a similar answer from Sasha, so I went with someone a bit younger.

"Toni?"

I pasted on a smile and nodded even though the newest nanny on the Elite Nanny Service roster couldn't see me. "Hey Molly. Are you busy tonight?"

"Kind of," she hedged. "I lost my new placement because the mom said I was too tempting or something stupid like that, so I'm trying to find a new wardrobe on a budget."

"Damn, I'm sorry Mols. Tonight I'm drinking, but I'll be happy to help you tomorrow."

"Really?" She gasped excitedly because I have the best fashion sense, period. "You sure?"

"Of course. As long as you realize nothing can cover up curves that spectacular." Molly needed to learn that her curves were not a statement on her sex life, despite what desperate housewives wanted her to believe. "But we'll tone it down as much as possible if that's what you want."

"It is."

"All right, see you tomorrow." I ended the call and stepped inside the dimly lit bar, finding an empty stool at the far end where I could be surrounded by people, but also be relatively alone. "Double whiskey. Neat, please."

I needed to get a new placement. Soon. I didn't do well with a lot of free time, especially after another interaction with my mother. She poked and judged until I lost my shit, and I hated that she knew the exact combination to make me lose my shit.

My next gig would be better, I told myself. It had to be better than a negligent workaholic who kicked me to the curb for daring to request a day off after working twenty-one straight days. The guy was an asshole, and if I never met another single parent like that again, it still wouldn't wipe away the nasty taste he'd left in my mouth.

Or maybe what I needed was someone to leave a nasty

taste in my mouth. I smiled to myself at the double entendre. Maybe I needed to get laid, and that would take my mind off things. But looking around the bar, all I saw were old timers who'd made drinking a profession, other sad bastards like me, and the young but poor crowd in search of one night of fun. *No, thank you.*

Yeah, I needed a new placement, and soon. Not because of the money, my trust fund made sure of that, but I needed to be busy. And if I didn't get one soon, maybe I would take off for a few months to a tropical island somewhere and work on my tan.

Oh yeah, that sounded perfect.

Chapter 3

Brady

"My philosophy is that kids are best when they are not seen. Or heard." Sarah, the latest interview to be Layla's nanny, not my next bedmate, purred the words through expertly lined lips and heavy lidded eyes. "Don't you agree, sir?"

My brows arched at the woman, grateful for my big oak desk as a barrier between us. "No, I don't agree at all. What are your qualifications?"

Sarah waved a dismissive hand in the air. "Oh, I have a kid of my own about the same age. I tell her to go to her room when mama needs some fun and she does. It works best for everyone."

Was this woman serious? "I'm in need of childcare and nothing else."

Her pink painted lips curled into what was supposed to be a sexy smile, but it only served to piss me off. "It's my experience that sometimes men don't know what they need. Sometimes, they need a little push in the right direction."

"Look Sarah, I only need someone to care for my niece and nothing else. Is that something you're interested in?"

She leaned back in her club chair, slowly crossing her legs to showcase them at their best. "Yeah, sure."

That was not the answer I was looking for. "Layla, can you come in here for a second?" It went against my better judgment to bring Layla into this, but I needed to give every candidate a proper chance. Right?

Layla walked in, her blond hair pulled into a bun on top of her head, dark jeans and t-shirt gave her a look of a child much older, but to me, she looked just like my sister. "What's up, Uncle Brady?"

"This is Sarah. She's interviewing to be your new nanny."

The look Layla gave Sarah made me smile. "Is she qualified?"

"Of course I'm qualified, Lola. Why else would I be here?" Her smile barely reached her eyes and she arched her back to show off a mediocre boob job.

Layla glared hard at Sarah, arching a brow as she studied her. "My name isn't Lola," she snorted and glared at me. "No. Not her. Anyone but her," she stated flatly, arms folded as she exited my office.

I don't bother to try for a sympathetic smile. "This isn't going to be a good fit." The woman was more interested in me than my niece. I was sure she didn't know who I was, but the house and the need for a nanny was a good indicator that I had money. "Thank you for your time."

Sarah stood, placing one knee on my desk and then the other, crawling across the large space until she was mere inches from my face. "It's probably for the best," she purred. "It's not good to mix business with pleasure."

My eyes bugged out of my head in disbelief. This was not real life. It couldn't be. I took a few steps back, shaking my head. "I'm afraid you don't understand."

"Oh, I understand all right. You're playing hard to get."

"No." Even if I was into playing games, which I wasn't, this wouldn't be one of them. I liked my games contained in the virtual world. "You need to leave."

She froze and then frowned. "You're serious?"

"I am." I quickly rounded the desk and headed for the front door, my strides long enough to put plenty of space between me and the ravenous babysitter. "Thank you for your time, Sarah."

"Your loss," she shot at me angrily, shrugging as she rushed out the front door.

At this rate I would never get this fucking game finished. I needed time, plenty of time. Hours of uninterrupted time to focus on all the fine details that would make my game stand out from all the other first person shooters on the market.

"It can't be this hard to find someone to watch my kid." I shook my head and went back to my office in search of a phone number I rarely used. A few years back when my company was just getting started, I did some freelance work for a big name gaming company and made friends with one of the players.

"Yo, Brady man, what's up? I thought you were dead." Alex Witter laughed heartily, the only way he knew how to laugh.

"Why would I be dead?"

"Because I invited you to my wedding. To my kid's birthday party and even a coed baby shower, and you didn't even say fuck off, that's why."

I frowned. "There have been some, ah, developments in my life that have required certain adjustments, which is actually why I'm calling."

"I'm listening."

I gave him a quick rundown of my sister's passing and the newest addition to my household. "I read about you falling in love with your nanny and I'm hoping you can recommend one for me?"

"To fall in love with?"

I rolled my eyes even though he couldn't see me. "Funny."

"Elite Nanny Service," he said and rattled off a number that I quickly jotted down. "She'll find you exactly what you need."

"Perfect. Thank you, Alex."

"Don't thank me. I'm planning an anniversary party for Sasha, and I expect you to be there. I won't take no for an answer," he said before ending the call.

I stared at the phone until the screen faded to black.

Alex was a decent guy, but he was far too gregarious and lively, which is why we almost never hung out, but the number he'd give me was worth considering his invitation. Maybe. If I managed to get a good Nanny.

"Elite Nanny Service, this is Serenity. How may I help you?"

"Oh, thank goodness. Ms. Woods, I was given your number by a friend, Alex Witter, and I'm in desperate need of a nanny. As soon as you can send one over."

There was a long silence on the other end of the line before the well-spoken, sultry voice responded. "That can be arranged," she said slowly.

"Oh, thank you! That's exactly what I needed to hear."

"But first I need you to come to my office for a proper interview."

My shoulders sank in disappointment. Of course this wasn't going to be easy. "You can't just send me a qualified nanny?"

"To a man I don't know and haven't vetted? Absolutely not." The woman sighed patiently. "It doesn't work that way, mister...?"

"Fine, I'll be at your office within the hour. Is that soon enough?"

"Yes," she said with a smile in her voice. "That works perfectly for me. See you then, mister?"

"Brady," I growled. "Call me Brady."

"I'll be waiting," she replied and ended the call.

As if I didn't already have a shit ton of tasks on my

plate, I now needed to leave my house and worse, I had to interact with people.

At least one person.

As far as I was concerned, that was one person too many. "Layla, get dressed! We have to go out for a bit."

Hopefully by the time we returned home there would be some plan for a nanny to start.

Soon.

Chapter 4

Toni

"Are you sure this is where I'm supposed to be, Serenity?" I sat in my car and stared up at the expansive brick mansion that was humongous but not ostentatious. Every detail I could see was functional and well-made, built for utility not for glamour. "This place could be a replica of my last placement." And that was the last thing I wanted to think about. Ever.

Serenity laughed, the sound husky yet feminine. "I'm sure. He's desperate and I think you are just what they need."

I rolled my eyes. "I'm not what anybody needs, but I'm good at my job."

"Be that as it may," she responded in that maternal voice that kept all the nannies in line, "Brady and his niece Layla could use someone with your particular skill set. And the address I gave you is accurate."

"Perfect. I'll let you know how it goes."

"I have no doubt this is the placement you've been searching for."

The smile in Serenity's voice put me on edge, and I blew out a long breath. "Anything else you can tell me? What he does for a living? What kind of hours I should expect?"

"Brady works at home so he will be there most days, but he'd rather keep the details under wraps."

I resisted the urge to roll my eyes once again. "As long as whatever he's into doesn't put me in any danger, it's fine with me."

"You'll be safe, Toni."

"All right, then. Wish me luck."

"Who needs luck when I have you?" Serenity ended the call and I sighed, staring at the oversized mansion until I gathered my thoughts enough to step out onto the long driveway and up to the imposing staircase.

It shouldn't be imposing, not when it's not as large as my own childhood home, but it felt like it was here for the sole purpose of intimidation. I didn't like it one bit, but I knew better than most how harmful it could be to judge a book by its cover. So I inhaled deeply, let it out slowly and rang the ornate brass doorbell twice.

Two minutes later the door opened and I really wished it hadn't. In fact, I wished I hadn't drank anything last night, because now I wasn't sure if the person standing before me was the person interviewing me or a whiskey induced fever dream.

He was gorgeous. No, that was too tame a word for the

sight of the man standing in front of me with thick chestnut brown hair and silver-blue eyes that were equal parts stormy and dreamy. He was tall, well over six feet, yet built. His corded forearms and strong hands said he was a man who took care of himself, but the disheveled wavy hair and steel-cut jawline gave him a roguish quality that I found irresistible.

Staring at the beautiful man made me happy that I'd dressed to impress. My red leather jacket hugged my body perfectly, and the black t-shirt, blue jeans with the skinny red belt, gave me the confidence boost I needed to go up against another so-called master of the universe. I tapped my red knee high boots impatiently and met his gaze head on.

"Are you Brady?" *Please, dear god let this be a brother or cousin and not the man I'm supposed to be working for.*

"Excuse me?" His dark brows furrowed in confusion.

I sighed deeply. "Brady. Is that you?"

He blinked until his beautiful icy blue eyes focused on my face. "Who are you?"

"My name is Toni. Serenity sent me for a two o'clock interview." I could already tell this was a man who didn't bother with niceties or details. He worked hard and that was it. "Are you Brady with no last name?"

He nodded absently, looking over my shoulder. "The interview isn't until two."

"Yeah, I know. It's ten minutes until two."

Brady stared at me with knitted, dark brown brows.

His pale gaze looked me up and down, assessing me carefully before his gaze landed on my face. "Okay."

"I'm here for the nanny position. Only the nanny position."

His lips twitched. "Come on in, Antonia."

"Toni," I corrected and stepped inside, ignoring the way his subtle, masculine scent worked its way into my nostrils before settling into my brain.

"Antonia is such a great name. Regal. Royal." He nodded for me to follow him and I did.

But I did not admire his long, lean runner's build. And I absolutely did not notice that his jeans fit as if he was sewn into them this morning. In fact, the moment we entered his office, I barely noticed him at all. The room was decorated in dark wood, black and brown leather with brass accents. It was a man's room, loaded up with books and computer equipment. "If you like the name, I'm happy to call you Antonia."

His lips curled into a grin. "Maybe the living room would be better," he said before turning and exiting his office, leading me back the way I came into the sparsely decorated living room. "So, Toni. Your qualifications are quite impressive."

Duh. "Thank you."

"How soon can you start?" His question was abrupt, and if coming from someone else, I might have felt suspicious, but I suspected he was just an abrupt kind of guy.

"Soon, but first we need to chat a bit more, don't you think?"

"Why? I need a nanny and you *are* a nanny."

I nodded slowly. "Parents who don't care about who takes care of their children, generally end up as problematic employers."

"Excuse me?"

I flashed a toothy grin, happy I'd gone for my bright red lipstick today. "What do you need from your nanny, Mr., ah Brady?"

He wanted to argue with me but thought better of it. "I need someone who knows children, someone who can work with a troubled little girl who is brilliant but struggling." He outlined her problems at school with a bully as well as her attitude towards her teachers. "She's a smartass, but only because she's incredibly smart. She's tough, and honestly far too mature for her years."

My smile softened. "She sounds incredible."

"She is, I think. But I'm not used to children and she needs help. I need a nanny who can help work on her social skills as well as her anger, but I also want to make sure she doesn't fall behind when she's allowed to start school again. It will require a one year commitment."

That was as close as a girl got to job security in this line of work. "Okay." Wow that was a lot of information in a short amount of time. "That's no problem. Anything else?"

"That about sums it up. Are you up for the challenge?"

"Sure. Can I meet her?"

He nodded, raking one hand through his thick, dark curls. "Layla."

A little blond girl appeared wearing black jeans, combat boots and a black and pink t-shirt that proclaimed her a clown wrangler. "You're the new nanny?"

I liked her right away. "Maybe. Depends on how we get along. You ever had a nanny before?"

"Nope. I went to school and hung out with my parents." She looked away at the mention of her parents and my heart ached for the little girl. Her gaze met mine again after a while. "I like your jacket."

"Thanks, I like your bracelets."

She smiled sweetly. "Can you cook?"

I shrugged. "Enough to get by. A big place like this doesn't have a cook?" It seemed odd but it wasn't my place to judge, at least not overtly.

Layla glared at her uncle with a look that clearly said, *"I told you so."*

"I told Uncle Brady the same thing. He can afford it, but he said no." Layla sighed like a long-suffering wall-flower and I couldn't help but smile. "He won't be happy until I burn the place down."

Brady let out a strangled noise that was difficult to decipher.

I bit back a laugh. "I'm nobody's version of Iron Chef, but I can teach you a few staples to avoid repeat visits from the fire department."

"Yeah?" Her silver-blue eyes shone with hope.

"Yeah, sure. It won't be fancy but it'll taste good and get the job done."

Layla studied me carefully, looking so much like her uncle minus the golden blond hair. "I like her," she declared and left the living room with a hint of a smile.

This was the strangest interview I'd ever been on, and I'd had tons of them over the course of my life, but it seemed like it was done. Brady stared at me before he wiped his hands on his thighs and stepped back.

"Can you start today? I'll double your rate for an entire shift if you say yes."

I resisted the urge—again—to roll my eyes at yet another rich dude who thought money was the only language they needed to know. "My normal rate will be just fine, Mr...Brady. But I will need to take a day off to pack up a few things sometime soon."

"Yeah, sure," he nodded but I could tell that his attention was already on whatever work he needed to do. "No problem." He stood, towering over me as he held out a hand to me.

I accepted the handshake, but I wished I hadn't when the jolt of electricity flooded my veins. It was visceral, the connection that swirled between us, which was ridiculous since I didn't even know his last name.

It's just physical, I told myself as I quickly shook his hand and yanked mine back, far out of his reach.

Far away from that uncomfortable feeling he evoked within me.

Far away from the urge to do something reckless. Something stupid.

Something dangerous.

Chapter 5

Brady

Progress.

Nothing felt better than two full days of uninterrupted work, tweaking code and making adjustments to the story, updating easter eggs and offering better bonus gifts. Day and night for the past forty-eight hours, my ass has been in my comfortable, plush, ergonomic office chair staring at three monitors until my vision started to blur. I didn't sleep, didn't rest and I didn't eat a thing until I felt I made enough progress to reward myself with basic human needs.

The best part was that Toni of the full red lips and ever-present leather jacket, had everything well in hand with Layla. She was confident and competent, and there hadn't been one damn smoke alarm in two full days.

A yawn cracked my jaw and I knew it was time to venture outside my office and into the rest of the house. After a much needed stop in the bathroom, my stomach roared with the ferocity of a Grizzly Bear and I realized day three was halfway over already, so I made my way to the kitchen. Before I had even taken a few steps in that direction, feminine laughter rang out. I got closer and heard music playing as well. It was a familiar song, one I'd heard hundreds, if not thousands of times during my youth.

"My mom loved this song," Layla said. There was a smile in her voice, and when my gaze landed on her, her expression was one of wistful happiness. For the first time in months she seemed lively. Really and truly happy, as evidenced by the wide smile that split her face. "The Ramones just do it right, she always said."

Toni was still shaking her round ass to the sound as she whipped her hair around, a smile on her face as well. "Your mom was right, and she had excellent taste in music."

I held my breath and waited for Layla's smile to fall, for the tears to come, but though her smile dimmed, it turned wistful. "She did. I miss her," she admitted quietly.

Toni stopped dancing as the music continued. "That's the part no one ever tells you, kiddo. The pain may lessen over time, but you'll always miss her. This song will play and you'll think of her. You'll see a bouquet of her favorite flowers and you'll want to buy them for her."

Before Layla could reply, the loud buzz of the oven timer interrupted whatever she'd been about to say and offered the perfect distraction.

Both females squealed excitedly and bent over at the same time to peek inside the oven.

"Do you think it's ready?" Layla's question was equal parts hesitant and excited.

Toni turned to her and even from my spot at the edge of the kitchen, I could see her cheeks spread into a smile. "There's only one way to find out. Do we risk it or be responsible and give it another few minutes?"

"Risk it!" Layla jumped up and down, smiling when Toni did the same.

"Okay girlie, back it up so I can get this beast out of here."

My niece gasped when the dish came out of the oven, her eyes as wide as her smile. "It's so big, Toni! It worked. It actually worked."

"Of course it did," she answered with an easy smile that drew me in as much as Layla. "We make a great team." With the dish in her hands, she set it on the cooling brick and that's when Toni spotted me. "We made a veggie and nut meatloaf. Hungry?"

"Starved," I admitted with a frown. "Are you vegan or something?" Nothing on her resume said she was, and I didn't really care, but Layla might not want to eat food without meat or dairy.

"No," she sighed as if she was disappointed in me. "But I do like vegetables and I think it's important to show the tiny humans just how great they can taste." Her gaze slid in Layla's direction as if to remind me of my charge.

"I love vegetables," Layla admitted. "Mom and Dad

said that vegetables are better for the environment so we only ate meat a couple times a week." Her eyes landed on mine, the accusation heavy in them and I couldn't blame her.

She's been here long enough that I should know those details. "Of course. Your mom made us all eat vegetarian for six weeks when she was fifteen."

"Are you joining us for lunch?" Toni arched a brow when I shook my head.

"No, I should get back to work," I said just as another loud roar sounded deep in my belly.

Layla laughed first and then Toni joined in as she grabbed another plate and handed it to Layla. "Broccoli and sweet potatoes on the side," she said easily as if I hadn't just refused her offer. "Sit."

I frowned. "You're bossy."

"Goes with the job," she said, handing me a big bowl of sweet potatoes and nodding towards the small table in the middle of the room.

"This looks good. Thank you for letting me crash your meal."

Toni shrugged like it was no big deal and Layla rolled her eyes, just in case I was starting to think things had changed between us. "It's your food, and I'm pretty sure you haven't eaten in a few days. Have you?"

"Uncle Brady is too busy and important to eat," Layla offered in a snide tone.

"Oh yeah? How important?" She arched her brows

and a playful smile formed on her lips as if she was teasing me.

"Not important," I rushed to answer before Layla told her who I was or what I did for a living. "Just incredibly busy right now."

Something that looked a lot like disbelief flashed in her bright green eyes and she turned her attention to her food. "Whatever you say."

"How long have you been a nanny?" Layla asked, seemingly content to pretend I don't exist.

"Six years, maybe seven at this point?" Toni thought about each answer as Layla fired them at her, it was a rare thing with most people. I couldn't keep my eyes off her.

The best part was that Layla's friendly interrogation gave me a chance to learn a lot about Toni without any effort. She obtained a master's degree in childhood development and early education in New York before she came to Texas for her first nanny gig. She's originally from the east coast and has a strained relationship with her parents. It wasn't much, but for some reason I was desperate to learn anything I could about her.

"What about you Layla, what do you do in your free time?"

She looked away, uneasy with the focus on her as she answered in a quiet voice. "I like to draw and I like to write stories."

"Like comic books or graphic novels?"

Layla's eyes went wide with excitement. "How did you know?"

"Writers who draw are a rare breed, my friend. I think it's incredibly cool, and if you ever want to share, I'd love to hear what you're working on." She stabbed a spear of broccoli and shoved it in her mouth, knowing that her easy acceptance of this hobby took the pressure off Layla.

She was, in a word, amazing. And more than that, her skills highlighted my own failures as I sat and listened, realizing that my niece was a complete stranger to me.

"Thanks," Layla muttered quietly and shoved a spoonful of potatoes in her mouth.

I ate a second helping of everything, and when I was done, I sat back and patted my belly. "Thank you, ladies. I really needed that." Eating for me was mostly about giving me enough fuel to keep working, but the meal was simple and delicious.

"No problem," Toni said and stood with a sigh.

My phone rang and I jumped to answer it, noticing the way Layla glowered angrily at the interruption.

"Hey Cal, what's up?" My creative director rarely called, which meant something was wrong. I stood and left the kitchen, well aware that I was letting my niece down.

Again.

Chapter 6

Toni

"Where are we going?" Layla's question put a smile on my face because she was an incredibly curious child. The best part was she didn't have any hangups about asking questions. It was a good trait for a youngster to have, as long as you weren't the person tasked with answering them all. I didn't have all the answers, hell I probably didn't' have most of them, but her curiosity made me want to find discover new things as well.

"We're almost there," I answered her question without really answering it.

"Okay," she smiled. "Are we going somewhere indoors or outdoors?"

I shrugged. "Yes."

"Toni," she whined. "Will there be food?"

"They have food, yes." I smiled again at her grunt.

"Are we going to watch something? To learn something?"

"Yes." I laughed at her impatient sigh. "We're almost there, little miss impatient."

"I don't really like surprises," she finally admitted. "The last time I was surprised, my mom and dad didn't come home."

"Shit," I blurted out. "Sorry. I mean *shoot*. That's totally my bad, Lay. This is a good surprise I promise, and if you don't like it when we get there we can do something else. No hard feelings. All right?" The little girl said nothing for a long time.

"Fine," she grumbled, a ghost of a smile appearing on her face.

When we arrived at the modern art museum, Layla was a little more cooperative. Her smile was hesitant, but she couldn't contain her excitement as we went from one exhibit to the next. We went through paintings and sketches, watercolors, charcoal and oil paints, and through it all Layla was exuberant and excited, practically vibrating with it. "This is really cool, Toni."

I couldn't conceal my smile at her happiness. "I think so too," I offered. "I've been to museums all over the world with my parents, and it was the best time I ever had with my folks." That was a sad indictment on my relationship with my parents, but it was the absolute truth. Dad didn't care as long as I was happy, but Mom treated every excursion like a final exam that took some—but not all—of the fun from every visit.

"My favorite time spent with Mom and Dad was traveling with them for work. They made homes that were good for the Earth," she said proudly. "I always went with them, but I was sick just before the last trip and they said I needed to stay home and get better." Layla looked away, her icy blue eyes filled with pain and regret. "I never got to see Norway," she replied with a choked smile.

My heart broke for this little girl, but I was an expert. "What was your favorite place to visit with your parents?"

"Mexico," she smiled widely. "There was this little cabin they built that was like living in a magic land. I wanted to stay there forever." The wistful smile on her face was contagious. I wrapped an arm around her as we walked from exhibit to exhibit, making sure she felt loved and protected.

"It sounds amazing, and I'm totally jealous." Sure I've been all over the world at my parents' side, but I never got to explore and enjoy the tourist spots unless they were on the schedule, which meant I got to see very little.

It took a few hours, but eventually we absorbed every exhibit inside the museum before taking a break for food and water, and a bathroom break. So far it was a good day, a great day even, and I felt like I was making progress with Layla. Progress that would help her heal going forward.

"Do you have a boyfriend?" Layla's question yanked a laugh out of me over lunch because it was so unexpected. Usually, in my experience, seven year olds weren't concerned with matters of love and romance.

I coughed to cover the laugh and shook my head. "No,

I don't. Boys and men are trouble, and I'm staying away from trouble for a little while." More like a good long while, but Layla was too young to be disillusioned with the reality of the male species. She didn't' need to know about my most recent ex-boyfriend who sent me to a spa for my birthday. Which upon first glance seemed like a thoughtful gift. But when I arrived, it was to discover that it was a weight loss spa, and instead of getting beauty treatments, he wanted me to fast and run and starve. I declined the diet portion of the weekend and overindulged in massages, masks and body wraps, taking full advantage of all the pampering packages throughout the weekend. When it was all over, I dumped him the minute I got back to town and I never looked back.

I shook off all thoughts of my past love life and smiled at Layla. "What about you, do *you* have a boyfriend?"

She giggled and it was the sweetest sound I'd heard in a long time, shaking her head even as laughter spilled out of her. "I'm too young for a boyfriend!"

"That's probably a good thing. Boys are trouble."

She giggled again. "Even Uncle Brady?"

Probably *especially* Uncle Brady with his nerdy good looks, premature curmudgeonly demeanor and sexy swagger. "Definitely Uncle Brady too."

Layla laughed again but soon enough her expression turned serious. "Do you think he likes having me here?"

Oh shit. "Your Uncle?"

She nodded.

"Yeah, I do. I mean it's an adjustment to get used to having a kid around, but I think he's learning."

She nodded, not quite believing me but desperately wanting to. "Okay."

I made a mental note to talk to Brady privately about making sure the little girl felt that she was wanted. I decided then and there that I would make sure Layla always felt wanted and loved, for as long as I was around. I leaned forward and flashed a smile.

"Layla, I have a very important question to ask you."

Her brows furrowed and her expression turned serious. "What is it?"

"How do you feel about tacos?"

The question caught her off guard just as I knew it would, and her little body shook with laughter once again.

Was there a better sound in this world than a kid's laugh?

In my experience, the answer was a resounding no.

Chapter 7

Brady

The doorbell rang and I jumped to my feet, rushing out of my office and to the front door before Toni could see my team arrive, and before Layla could let my identity slip. Why it mattered that she didn't know who I was, I couldn't quite say, except I liked that Toni treated me like just another man. She didn't defer to me because of my wealth, hell she didn't even defer to me based on my status as her employer. And I liked it.

A lot.

I yanked open the door to see the heads of my major teams. Sierra, the head of marketing, was a thirty-something year old woman with hot pink hair. Cal, my creative director, wore black thick framed glasses, hoodies and jeans just about every day. Tori the lead designer, was the most normal of the bunch in jeans, a button up shirt, and occasionally a jacket.

"Morning guys, come on in." I waved them in quickly, looking over my shoulder like a teenager having guests over when he wasn't supposed to.

Sierra stepped in first. "Mr. Winsome," she began and I cut her off.

"Call me Brady," I spoke over her before she could say anything else.

Sierra's brows knitted into a frown but she shrugged. "Sure, okay *Brady*. Whatever you say. Where should we set up?"

"Follow me," I instructed, glad that I was the boss. No one said anything about my insistence on keeping things informal today, and if they thought it was odd, they kept it to themselves, a fact for which I was grateful. I kept my head down and powered through the living room, but the keen scent of warm butter brought me up short in the middle of the kitchen. "Dammit," I whispered more to myself than the group behind me.

"Oh hey, you're just in time for...oh, a party." Toni flashed a stunningly wide smile at the group. "Good morning...people. Anyone hungry?" She aimed a spatula at my employees, still smiling.

"I could eat," Cal said automatically, no doubt hypnotized by the sight of Toni in black leather leggings, a dark blue shirt with a delectable vee and bright blue sneakers. Or maybe, like me, he was taken in by the painted red mouth.

"Me too," Tori added with a surprised smile.

"I can always eat," Sierra offered with a smile before her gaze landed on me. "Or...not?"

"Nonsense," I added, trying like hell to keep the anger out of my voice. "Eating now means we can power through for a few hours." At least for them. My mind, however, would be firmly stuck on the sight of Toni's curves in those damned leggings.

"Cool." Toni didn't miss a beat, pointing towards the table where Layla sat quietly reading on her tablet. "That's Layla."

Layla looked up as if she suddenly realized the kitchen was full of adults. "Oh, hi. Good morning. Who are you?"

They all laughed before introducing themselves one by one. "We work for, um, with Brady." Cal frowned as if the words felt strange on his lips before he shrugged and sat.

An hour later everyone had full bellies and wide smiles as they profusely thanked Toni for breakfast, and—finally—we departed for the confines of my office.

"No wonder you're so relaxed," Cal joked the minute the door closed behind us.

"She's the nanny," I growled, shutting down any hint of gossip before it could get started.

"Right," he muttered under his breath. "A hot rich nerd ends up with a nanny like that and keeps it strictly platonic. And I'm Elon Musk."

I glared at him while Tori and Sierra roared with laughter. "Funny. Put that creative thinking towards the game."

Cal snickered to himself and shrugged as he fired up his laptop and started working along with the rest of us.

For the next few hours we worked like a well-oiled machine, only stopping to collaborate on this item or that, making more progress in six hours than we'd made in the past three months. I was glad for the marathon work session even though it didn't keep my mind off the distracting nanny.

Did she have to be so fucking bubbly and bright? She was hard to ignore. And those curves? Was I some sort of warlord in a previous life and she was my punishment in this one? Her and those mouthwatering curves that seemed to go on forever. I couldn't even sleep knowing she was just a few doors down, wondering what she slept in? Did she wear those skimpy lacy things women thought men wanted, or was she a straight to the point woman who slept in the buff? "Fuck," I growled.

"Something wrong, boss?" Sierra didn't even try to hide her smile, and even though it annoyed me, I bit back my words and focused on my monitors.

"Nope. Nothing," I shot back quickly, refusing to think about the sleepless nights caused by the nanny and the long showers where I imagined her doing all manner of filthy things to me, and me to her. "Nothing at all."

"It's good to know he's human," Cal offered with a sympathetic smile. "I'd have a hard time concentrating with a beauty like that around. Red hair is my weakness," he admitted, never taking his eyes off his own laptop.

I frowned but it wasn't with anger or even embarrassment. I felt like one of the group, as if we were—in a way—commiserating over something universally relatable. "She works for me."

Sierra sighed. "Considering how much most of us work, where the hell else are we supposed to meet people?"

That was a good point, one I hadn't considered. Thankfully the sound of a small but powerful knock on the office door stopped that line of conversation.

"Enter." I steeled myself to see Toni again, but it was Layla who poked her head in.

"Hi. Lunch is in the kitchen if you're hungry!" She ducked out and the sound of her fading footsteps was all that was left of my niece.

"Cute kid," Sierra said. "No wonder you've been distracted. There's a lot going on here lately."

"I'm working on it," I bit out harshly.

"No judgment," she offered. "It's a lot to take on, and now it makes sense. We all thought you were burnt out maybe. Glad to see it's just normal life shit."

I frowned. "Why didn't you just ask?"

She laughed. "You're not exactly the sharing personal deets kind of guy, *Brady*." Her emphasis on my name wasn't lost on me.

Had I really not told my employees that I was now guardian to my niece? That my sister and brother-in-law had died? Most of the time I work in my home office, leaving my COO to run the office. It was an arrangement that had worked well for years, so I had never needed to share much of my personal life with the staff before now. But maybe I sold myself short as well as them? "Let's break for lunch," I said and glanced down at my phone. "Or an early dinner."

"Food anytime of day is good," Cal replied with a smile as he made a quick exit.

There was no hint of Layla or Toni in the kitchen. I found a note written in neat cursive telling me they'd gone to the park for some outdoor time and that Layla helped make the sandwiches. There were more sandwiches than four people could eat, plus chips, cheese puffs, salad and a platter of antipasto.

"Whoa, fancy stuff here," Sierra laughed and plucked a sundried tomato from the platter, groaning as she chewed it. "I say we make this a working lunch," she began with a conspiratorial smile. "To make sure we make the most of their hard work," she added with a laugh.

I ignored the pang of disappointment that washed over me when I read Toni's note, clutching it in my hand like it was a Dear John letter. "Yeah, a working lunch sounds good."

We worked through lunch and the early evening. I was satisfied that we were all caught up and back on track when I closed the door behind my team.

Progress.

It felt good to finally have some semblance of control over at least one aspect of my life.

Since I had not one fucking iota of control over my thoughts where a certain fire haired nanny was concerned.

Chapter 8

Toni

The one thing I missed about living in an apartment since leaving my family home was having a nice place to curl up under the stars and get lost in a fascinating story. Sure, as a nanny I was often living in a large home just like this one, but so many families have no concept of personal time. If you show your face during off-the-clock hours, then you couldn't have a moment of peace. The kids looked to you as the authority figure in their lives because you were there for them, and the parents were out of their depth and expected the nanny to pitch in out of the goodness of her heart.

That shit was tiring, so I got used to reading in my room.

But Brady, *no last name,* wasn't that much of a stickler, and he spent every waking hour in his office, so once Layla was down for the night I knew I could come out here and read in peace. And the reading *would* have been peaceful if I didn't keep imaging the sexy cop from my novel with Brady's long-legged, lazy gait and his sexy smile. The man rarely smiled, but when he did—holy crap—it was a thing of beauty. His full lips spread into an almost picture-perfect smile highlighted by straight white teeth and that ever present hint of stubble that I could practically feel on the insides of my thighs.

"You didn't have to make lunch today."

I nearly jumped out of my skin at the sound of Brady's deep voice. Slowly I turned to look over my shoulder, trying with everything in me to pretend as if I wasn't just thinking about his face buried between my thick thighs.

"Brady." My voice came out breathless, and I cleared my throat and tried again. "Did I overstep?" I knew there were some people, mostly women, who objected to any move that would make it seem as if they weren't super-women who could lead board meetings and whip up lunch for a crowd.

His dark brows pulled into a frown and he shook his head. "What? No. Absolutely not. I'm grateful for your thoughtfulness, I just wanted you to know that it isn't expected of you. It's not part of your job description, so while it's very much appreciated and always appreciated, it isn't required." He looked so sincere it was hard to look away, especially with the way his blue eyes searched my face.

And then lower.

I felt his gaze deep in my belly before the hot flushed

feeling worked its way down between my thighs. *Dammit, no Toni. No lusting after the sexy, nerdy, single dad.*

I tried for a smile that I hoped was friendly and professional. "You guys seemed busy, and Layla mentioned that you tend to forget to eat. We made math problems out of it if that makes you feel better."

His broad shoulders relaxed. "It does. A little. Thank you, Antonia."

Why was it that when Brady called me Antonia it didn't feel too formal, too stuffy and rigid? It must be the deep timbre of his voice, the smooth whiskey sound compared to my mother's disapproving tone. Yeah, that had to be it.

"Toni," I reminded him out of habit more than any desire for him to call me by my nickname.

"Right. Sorry." His long legs brought him forward so we were side by side when he dropped down into the lounger beside me. "Are you settling in all right?"

I turned away from his handsome face and tilted my head up, taking advantage of the view of the stars that twinkled above us in a beautiful light display that felt like it was just for me.

"Yep. Layla is a great little girl. She's more mature than any seven year old I've met, and much smarter. But there's still a little girl in there." She was still hurting from losing her parents, but that wouldn't go away anytime soon.

"No kidding," he sighed and scrubbed a hand over his

face. "Some days she sounds like a teenager. A sullen, angsty teenager."

I laughed at his totally accurate description of his niece. "Like I said, mature for her age. But," I turned to face him and immediately wished I hadn't, because his gaze was focused on my face, full of heat and hunger and… wait, that can't be right.

"But?" His lips pulled up into a crooked grin that was utterly irresistible.

"But you might be happy to learn that I don't think it's because she lost her parents. She spent a lot of time with adults when she traveled with them." The little girl had lived a full life already and it was awe-inspiring.

"She talks to you a lot," he said, the words were not an accusation but merely a statement of fact.

"I'm easy to talk to," I shot back easily. "And she misses having people to chat with since she's not in school."

"Right," he winced as if I'd slapped him.

"It's not a judgment, I swear. Just an observation."

"She seems to like you more than she likes me."

I flashed a wide, playful grin. "I'm a likeable kind of gal."

Brady laughed, shaking his head as if he found me amusing, possibly endearing. "That you are, Toni. How do you do it?"

I laughed. "I don't know. Part of it is just my upbringing I guess, always be polite and well-mannered.

That combined with growing up as an only child gave me the required confidence to just be me."

His brows rose. "Just like that?"

"Not quite. It took me some time to find myself and even longer to own it."

His gaze intensified as if I was a puzzle he needed to figure out. "You seem pretty comfortable in your skin to me."

"I am, but I wasn't always." I sighed, laying back so my focus was back on the stars. "I was expected to be something I'm not, including thin and quiet."

"I think you look great," he said almost automatically. "And quiet is overrated. This place was too quiet before you came around, and I'm not sorry about the change."

Holy shit, was that a compliment? I laughed nervously at his unintentionally kind words. "Thank you?"

He smiled again and I was grateful I was already sitting, because my knees went a little weak at the sight of his smile.

"You're welcome." He looked up at the sky and sighed. "You really think Layla is all right?"

I nodded. "Yes. She's sad and working her way through her grief, but yes, I think she's doing fine. Other than the getting kicked out of school thing."

"Yeah," he sighed, the weight of the world on his broad shoulders. "I'm failing her, aren't I?"

"No, but I think you should make time for her. She needs to know she's loved and not just an obligation."

He sat up. "Did she say something to you?"

"Not directly." I turned to face him and our gazes collided, sending a wave of fire through me that made me gasp. "But, she thinks you don't want her here."

Brady looked at me with hurt filled eyes as if I was accusing him, and I wanted to reach out, to smooth the frown from his brows and wipe away the pain my words caused.

"It's not that," he began and shook his head.

"Brady, I know."

"How can you possibly know that?"

"Because I lived that life." It wasn't something I shared freely, but for some reason I wanted to ease his pain. "My parents sent me to boarding school when I was Layla's age, said it would teach me what I needed to learn to survive in the world. What they meant was, in *our* world."

"*You* went to boarding school?"

I laughed. "You don't have to sound so surprised. I wasn't meant to be the society wife type though, and I'm fine with that."

"It's not that, it's just," he trailed off, shaking his head, but I didn't need him to finish what he was going to say. I'd heard it plenty of times over the past few years.

"It's just why would I choose to be a nanny when I could be anything else?"

Surprise flashed in his eyes. "Yeah."

"This is what I wanted to do." It was as simple and as complicated as that. The longer Brady stared at me, the more uneasy I felt, and it wasn't that anxious kind of unease, it was the sexual tension type. The kind that had me squeezing my knees together and ignoring the tightening of my nipples in my bra, the way my belly quivered. I stood quickly, maybe a little too quickly to be graceful. "I should, uh, go to bed."

Brady stood, a hint of a smile on his lips as if he knew what I was doing. "I'll walk you up."

"No need," I stammered. "I know the way."

He flashed another killer smile and nodded towards the door. "So do I."

Knowing I was beat, I nodded and moved past him, making my way inside. The house was dark and quiet, the tension swirled around me and Brady, thick and heavy. I sucked in a near silent deep breath and let it out slowly as we began to climb the carpeted stairs.

This is just my boss being kind, nothing else. The heat between us is only in my mind. It's not really happening. The heat of his body against my back was like eating chocolate and oysters while downing a saucer of absinthe all at once. Or something similar.

My legs slowed as the door came into view and I urged them forward. *This isn't me waiting for some end of date kiss* —which I haven't done in ages—*this is my boss walking me to my room.* My attempt at rationalizing the situation didn't help, not when he was so close, so masculine. So potent.

"This is me," I said, attempting to sound easy and breezy.

Brady smiled. "Thanks for the chat, Antonia."

Yep, there went that flutter low in my belly again. "Toni," I whispered back breathlessly.

"Right," he whispered and stepped closer. "Toni. You feel like an Antonia to me." His warm breath fanned against my face and his smile worked its way down my spine and curled around my waist. And then his hands curled around my waist and pulled me flush against him. His heart thudded against his chest, his body was hard everywhere. *Everywhere.*

"And how exactly does an Antonia feel, Brady?"

"Like this," he growled and pressed his lips against mine, letting his tongue swing back and forth across the seam of my lips. "And this," he said with a smile as he let the tip of his tongue trace the shape of my lips.

Had any man ever caused such a reaction with just a kiss?

"And this," he growled as his hands slid down from my waist and gripped my ass at the same time his tongue slipped into my mouth. Brady explored the depths of my mouth, the dark, wet recesses and the different textures of my tongue. They danced together, polite at first and then hungry, and then so intense that I felt every drop of my blood as it rushed through my veins.

This was what a kiss was meant to be. Hot and fast, and so out of control it made your head spin. It made you forget what the smart thing to do was, it made you forget your own damn name. Everything but how to enjoy the moment and that's what I decided to do, enjoy this impromptu make out session with my hot boss.

My skin was hot and flushed, my panties were soaked and his big, capable hands were the only things keeping me on my feet. I leaned into him and let my hands roam his body, feeling every hard plane and ridge of his chest and abs, down his strong back and firm ass. *Holy fuck, Brady the nerd is ripped!*

Brady the nerd.

That thought jolted me out of the kiss-induced stupor and I pulled back. I didn't know this man, not really. I knew his first name was Brady and he did something with computers. I knew he cared for his niece after her parents died, but that was it. No last name, nothing important other than how his body felt beneath my hand.

This is the definition of a bad idea, I told myself and took a step back. "I should, um...good night."

He smiled, and it was as if the kiss never ended because I could still feel his mouth on mine, his tongue devouring me. "Good night, Antonia."

I opened my mouth to remind him that my name was Toni, but Brady put two fingers to my lips.

"I like Toni," he purred. "But I like Antonia better."

Holy. Shit. My tongue slipped out and slid against his fingertips and he pulled back as if my tongue had burned him. "Good to know." With that I slipped into my bedroom and closed the door, pulse racing wildly at the hot as fuck exchange.

I enjoyed the moment. Enjoyed the memory of his mouth on mine and his hands on my body. Enjoyed the heavy lidded, lust filled look in his eyes when I licked his fingers.

And then I proceeded to freak the fuck out.

Chapter 9

Brady

Saturday morning arrived far too soon, but it was quiet, almost silent, as if I'm being punished for keeping my distance from Toni after that magnificent kiss that has plagued my thoughts and memories for the past few days. That kiss, the one that had sent me straight to the shower to take care of the aching weight in my balls.

I needed to keep my distance, I had to, because Toni worked for me and no matter what Sierra said, it was a recipe for disaster.

It had to be.

Right?

Even though I'd had a few days of distance, thoughts of her still stuck with me. The taste of her, the feel of her under my hands, it was all I thought about. It was becoming damn inconvenient, the way she weighed on my mind, plagued my thoughts like some kind of sorceress who had gripped me in her spell.

"Stop it," I ordered and sat up in bed, looking around my darkened bedroom to make sure life as I knew it was still the same. Toni wasn't beside me in bed, her curves weren't pressed up against me and there was no lingering warmth to say she'd been here, which meant I needed to get my head screwed on straight.

Toni was. Never here, she was just on my mind. But today wasn't about her, today was about...Layla.

"Shit." It was the weekend and my plan had been to spend some quality time with my niece. Listening to Toni tell me that Layla felt unwanted had stuck with me, and it was on me—and no one else—to change her perception. That meant I had to get my shit together. Take a shower. Get dressed. Make a plan.

I would do all of that, as soon as I eased my mind of thoughts of Toni, which maybe included rubbing one out to the thought of those magnificent curves under my hand, her pliant kisses and soft moans that kept me hard for hours, days on end. Thirty minutes later I felt mostly human as I emerged from the shower dressed in jeans and a t-shirt, ready to spend a day with a seven year old.

Layla was, of course, in the kitchen with a bowl of granola, yogurt and fresh fruit in front of her. She had her tablet in hand as well. She looked up at me without a hint of emotion.

"Morning, Uncle Brady."

I didn't flinch at her subdued greeting, instead I

smacked a smile on my face. "Good morning, Niece Layla. How's it going?"

She looked up at me as if I'd lost my mind. "Um, fine?"

Okay. I wasn't expecting a complete one-eighty after months of neglect, but I also wasn't deterred. "Fine is a good start, but I think we can do better than that. What would you like to do today?"

She froze with her spoon halfway between her bowl and her mouth. "Do?" Layla nodded at her tablet with a frown. "Read, and maybe draw while you work. I'll stay out of your way. Promise."

At those words I did flinch. Was I really such a tyrant she thought I couldn't be bothered at all? *Yes*, my conscience answered quickly. "Not today you won't. And for the record, you aren't a bother. Sometimes I just get lost in my work and forget about the world around me because I've never had to think about anyone else. But I'm working on it, okay?"

"Sure," she shrugged.

"Today you and I are going to spend some time together, get to know each other. So I think you need to figure out what you want to do."

Her blond brows furrowed deep in thought. "Mom always said that Texas has the best barbecue."

"That's a fact I can tell you is absolutely true," I laughed and shook my head. "Our first meal will definitely be good old-fashioned Texas barbecue. Anything else?"

She shook her head. "Toni and I have visited a few museums, but I don't know what else I want to do."

I nodded and looked around the kitchen as an idea struck. "Okay, well, do you like sports?"

She looked up at me with a question in her silver blue eyes. "Maybe?"

"All right, then I know what our first stop is going to be."

Two hours later we sat in box seats at the stadium for the Houston Highlanders. Layla had wide smile on her face as the players skated out onto the ice. "You like hockey Uncle Brady?"

I shrugged. "I know one of the players. We did some work together and have stayed in touch. On and off," I admitted.

"You must be Brady Winsome." A pretty woman with big blue eyes and a giant pregnant belly smiled at me and then down at Layla. "I'm Sasha."

"Alex's wife," I said as my memory returned. "Congratulations on the nuptials and the baby."

"Thanks," she laughed. "I'm surprised you found your way out for a game. Alex will be pleased."

I frowned. "He will?"

She rolled her eyes. "Of course, he loves to show off on the ice. It's unlikely you'll beat him on real life ice," she said, likely referencing the ass whooping I dished out when we were testing the hockey game that bears his face.

I laughed. "Without a doubt," I said and introduced her to Layla.

"Nice to meet you, Layla. Are you a hockey fan?"

"Don't know yet," she answered honestly, but an hour

into the game, she was yelling and banging on the windows of the box as she shouted at refs for what she perceived as bad calls. "This is pretty cool, Uncle Brady." Her smile was better than any praise.

"You're a born hockey fan," I told her as the game ended with the Highlanders up by three goals.

"It was fun," she said with a shrug as we made our way down the tunnel to meet with Alex.

He strolled out of the locker room with a cocky smile and a strong handshake for me. "Brady, man, I'm glad you made it. Finally." His gaze landed on Layla. "Who is this?"

"I'm Layla," she answered and extended a hand. "Uncle Brady is my uncle and now my dad. Sort of."

Alex's brows raised in question and I nodded my confirmation. "I lost my sister and brother-in-law more than a year ago."

"Shit man, I'm sorry to hear that."

"He said shit," Layla said without much emotion.

Alex roared with laughter. "Maybe we should start an unexpected fathers club." He shook his head and shook Layla's hand. "It is great, though, isn't? These little humans will keep you on your toes."

I hadn't thought of it like, that but as we said our goodbyes and made our way to the best barbecue restaurant in Houston it was all I could think about. Toni seemed taken with Layla, and Alex seemed to feel the same about his kids, which led me to believe that I was missing something.

"I hope you're hungry, Lay."

"Yep," she admitted as we walked inside the dimly lit

restaurant with a large, dark wooden bar and leather booths lining the walls. "What's your favorite?"

"I don't have one. Usually I eat something quick, but I'm always a fan of barbecue chicken. And ribs."

Her gaze scanned the menu carefully. "How about a sampler? We can share and try everything."

"That's a good idea," I told her. "But I'm really hungry so maybe we should order two?"

"That's a lot of food, Uncle Brady."

"True, but we can eat any leftovers for dinner. How does that sound?"

Her smile beamed and she looked just like my sister. "Okay."

We placed our orders and I allowed myself to relax minute by minute, getting to know my niece as a person rather than just another obligation. She drank her lemonade and I enjoyed a cola, silence danced around us.

"Why won't you tell Toni who you are?" Her gaze met mine head on and she smiled. "She's really smart and knows something is up with you."

My brows furrowed of their own volition at her astute observation. She was right, of course. I was keeping my true identity from Toni, mostly out of habit. When people in general—women specifically—found out who I was, they changed. They were suddenly more polite and solicitous, more forgiving of my bad habits, and so fucking nice it made me want to scream. I hated it, but Toni didn't do that. Most of the time when she looked at me there was a mix of annoyance and heat in her gaze. She wasn't impressed by me for the simple act of having money because it seemed like she grew up with a certain amount of wealth.

"I know she does," I admitted. "But I like that she likes me without knowing who I am."

"Does she really know you then?"

I barked out a laugh. "You really are too smart for your own good."

She shrugged, sitting back when our gigantic order arrived. "She likes who she thinks you are, but she's gonna be mad when she finds out, and she will find out."

Her words echoed inside of my chest like a warning sign. "You're so sure she will find out?" She might be a little miffed, but I figured this was where Layla's naivete took over.

"Mom always said that lies can only live in the dark but sometime soon the sun will rise and expose them."

Dammit Marnie for raising such an incredible child. "How did you get to be so smart?"

"I read a lot," she answered with a wide smile. "And Mom and Dad said every moment was a learning opportunity."

"That sounds a lot like Marnie." My sister made sure that every experience opened your eyes to something new, whether it was watching a turtle cross the road on its own, or a difficult math problem. "I hope you apply that same maturity when you return to school."

Layla rolled her eyes. "Uncle Brady."

"I'm serious. "No matter how big an asshole someone is, you can't hit them." No matter how much you want to.

She smiled. "You said asshole."

I laughed at my misstep and pointed at my smiling niece. "If you say that word at school, I will take away all of your devices for six months. At least."

Instead of frowning, she giggled and it was the sweetest sound I'd ever heard. "Deal," she finally answered and struck her hand out for me to shake, which I did with the same vigor I used to close any deal. "I didn't hit her right away," she explained. "She kept saying stuff every single day. Mocking me for being new and my new clothes, for reading all the time. I let it slide like Mom always said. And then she made fun of me, saying I was so horrible my parents died to get away from me, and I lost it."

"Ah, fuck, kiddo." What kind of trash kid would say such an awful thing. "I'm sorry she was such a little asshole." I truly was, but this was a learning opportunity. "She deserved that punch, however I'll deny ever saying that, but," I sighed because I needed her to understand something she was far too young to have to understand. "But the thing is Layla, you don't deserve the punishment you've been forced to serve. Ya know?"

She nodded and looked away nervously. "So I just have to take it?"

"No, you just have to keep your hands to yourself. The best revenge is to take her down a peg and to do it publicly. It works on pretty much all bullies."

"You were bullied?"

I nodded, reluctant to go back to that time in my life, but for Layla I had to. "I was. Your mom was my biggest defender, but she left for college and then the real world when I was pretty young. So I had to learn to handle them on my own." I refused to tell her how I hacked the grades of my bullies to make them attend summer school or worse, ineligible to play homecoming games as payback. "I got successful and now they wall want to be me or work for me, which is pretty sweet revenge."

She laughed, her barbecue smeared smile wide. "You're like an evil villain, Uncle Brady."

It was my turn to laugh at her assessment. "No, just a desperate bullied kid who used my skills to better my life. That's what I want for you, Lay. It's what Marnie would have wanted too."

She nodded and leaned forward with an evil smile on her face. "Maybe I'll steal her boyfriend or worse, her best friend!"

I froze for a moment before laughter took over. "I want to be terrified of that comment, but the truth is I'm kind of proud."

Layla preened before she reached for a spare rib, shoving it in her mouth and followed up with a handful of French fries.

"Thank you," she said around a mouthful of food.

"You're going to give me premature gray hair, aren't you?"

Her smile faded into a fake innocence as she shook her head. "Me? No. Never."

Chapter 10

Toni

Sitting in traffic on my way back to Brady and Layla felt odd. Surreal, even. I spent the entire weekend burning out half a dozen batteries to thoughts of the hot nerd whom I didn't really know, and doing something I never do, daydream about the cutie. What in the hell kind of spell had he woven around me that I'd spent the weekend inside my apartment instead of hitting the bars and finding a hookup buddy?

"Ugh, gross," I growled as a guy in a shiny red pickup truck flicked his tongue out at me suggestively and wiggled his brows. "I don't think so, dirtbag." I flipped the guy off and gunned it at the green light until he was just a speck in my rear view mirror.

The mansion looked the same as I had when I pulled away on Friday evening, putting as much distance as I could between me and Brady. That kiss had stayed with me for far too long. The truth was, it still lingered on my lips and in the deep, dark recesses of my mouth. I wanted the promise that kiss offered, but I also knew I couldn't have it.

Wouldn't.

It wasn't just dangerous to my heart, it was also a professional risk.

Yeah, I couldn't risk it, so instead I took my frustrations out on my vibrators, coming to the feel of his mouth and body on me all weekend long. Hmm, maybe I need to invest in some rechargeable devices, cuz living under the same roof with Brady days a week will give me all kinds of ideas.

"No time for that, Toni." I gave myself a mental pep talk as I drove up the long driveway and shifted my car into park. "This is my job. Work. Not a dating site or a hookup app. Work."

I stepped inside the house and it was relatively quiet given that a seven year old lived here. I crept inside to avoid alerting anyone—mostly Brady—to my presence. It was useless though, because halfway up the staircase the sound of small footsteps drew my gaze to the top of the steps. "Hey, Layla."

She flashed a happy smile. "Hi Toni. I finished my story. Wanna read it?" Her expression was so eager and excited with a pinch of hesitation that it made my heart squeeze. "If you don't want to," she began but I stopped her.

"Of course I do. Hand it over, little girl." I held out my hand with a grin.

"You sure?"

I nodded. "I am. Are you?"

"No," she admitted easily.

"All the more reason you have to give it to me, then. Art is terrifying for the *artiste*."

She laughed, shoving it at me before she took off, as if I could read it quick enough to give her feedback in the next five seconds.

I smiled at her retreating form and I realized that I missed Layla this weekend. She was a sweetheart who hadn't let the world get her down, no matter how hard it seemed to try.

I made my way to my room where I took my time unpacking and tidying up the place. After a quick, hot shower, I changed into comfortable loungewear before I curled up on the bed to read Layla's story. It was smart and engaging, and it felt as if it was written by a far more mature and experienced storyteller. I couldn't help but cry as I came to the end of the tale.

"I have to tell her how good it is. Now."

I rushed from my room, barefoot and disheveled, in search of the budding artist, but it seemed as if she had disappeared. "Layla!" She didn't answer and I jogged down the stairs, searching the media room and even the pantry, but she wasn't anywhere to be found. "Lay?"

My gaze landed on Brady at the grill with a long silver spatula in his hand. He wore a plain white t-shirt that hugged all of his muscles perfectly. His biceps bunched and flexed with every move and his back muscles danced against the shirt as he flipped burgers and steaks on the grill. "Toni, you're home."

Home. Had any place ever been home for me? There were plenty of places over the years where I rested my head, but none I considered home, just a place that I lived.

"I'm here," I said with a small smile.

"Come on back." He waved me over like we were old friends, worse, like he was happy to see me. "How was your weekend?"

"Uneventful," I lied because you couldn't exactly tell a man that you spent all weekend dreaming about him doing dirty, wicked things to you while your battery operated boyfriend made you come over and over again. "Yours?"

Heat flared in his eyes as if he spent the weekend doing the same thing. "Pretty similar. Hungry?"

I shook my head. "Nah, I don't want to intrude. I was just looking for Layla."

He arched his dark brows, lips tugged into a knowing smile. "You don't want to know about the hockey game we attended together? Or the long conversation we had over Texas barbecue?" He shrugged. "I thought you might."

I rolled my eyes. "Coy isn't a good look on you."

"No? You should see me naked. That's a good look on me." He winked at my shocked expression and I suppressed the shiver that rolled down my spine.

"Well now you've got my interest piqued."

Heat flared in his gaze again and he licked his lips. "Good."

Over lunch, Layla and Brady recounted their weekend

of bonding together and I found myself smiling the whole time. They were cute now that they were getting used to one another. "Sounds like a good time."

"It was," Layla said, still beaming from my praise of her book. "Can I go to my room now, Uncle Brady? I want to work on my next story."

He nodded, a wistful smile on his face as he watched her dart up the stairs. "I've created a little workaholic."

I laughed. "Monkey see, monkey do?"

His eyes crinkled adorably at the corners. "All I hear you saying is that I've created a monster."

I laughed again, this time louder. "Imitation is the sincerest form of flattery?"

Brady laughed as he stood, grabbing two fresh beers and handing me one of them. His expression cleared of all amusement as he studied my face. "Do I need to apologize for the kiss?"

"No," I cocked a brow. "But if you need to apologize for anything you can apologize for avoiding me."

He nodded and his overgrown hair fell over one eye. "I had to in order to avoid doing something dangerous, like kissing you again. Or more. But I'm sorry."

"Good."

Surprise flashed in his eyes. "So, why did you stop the kiss when it was just getting good?"

My eyes bugged out of my head. *Was that kiss just getting good? As in, it got better than that?* My skin flushed at the thoughts that ran through my head. "Because I don't know you, Brady, not really. And the things that I do know, namely that you're my employer, makes taking this attraction any further a bit complicated."

He listened closely and nodded thoughtfully. "Whatever objections you have, please know that your job is safe."

I wanted to believe that, but I wasn't a naïve little girl who believed the easy thing. "Things don't always work out that way when emotions are involved."

Brady nodded thoughtfully as if he was really listening and giving my words proper consideration. "You're doing a great job with Layla and that's what is most important to me. She's lost so much already, and she really cares about you, Toni. The job is yours for as long as you want it."

Again, I wanted to believe him, but I couldn't, so I ignored the relief that plowed through my body at his words. To be honest, the relief I felt at his seemingly sincere words pissed me off. I wasn't some shrinking flower, I wasn't a swooning type of woman who got giddy over a few pretty reassurances.

"Good to know."

His gaze never left my face, as if he was trying to read my thoughts. "What's your real objection?"

I stared at him with an expression that said *seriously?* But he still didn't get it, I sighed heavily and shook my head. "My objection is that I don't know you, Brady."

"You want to know me," he said in a tone that was a step below devastated.

"Is that so bad?" Maybe it was. Maybe he had some deep dark secrets he was afraid I'd learn if he slept with someone who lived in his home. "Right. Look if you don't want to tell me about yourself, I can handle it." I stood, staring at Brady's face for a long minute as I waited for an answer.

He stared back, those silver blue eyes looked tortured and pleading, but I refused to read anything into what I thought I saw.

"Good night, Brady." I took my beer upstairs to my room and called Lucy to tell her just how badly I screwed up. "It was a mistake, and I'm pretty sure this job is only going to last another few weeks."

Lucy was silent for a long time and I knew this meant she was trying to figure out how to say what was on her mind. "Do you think it was stupid of me to sleep with Dante?"

"At first I did, but it became obvious pretty quickly that you guys were more than a few stolen fucks."

She laughed. "Thanks, I think." Lucy laughed again. "It *was* stupid, and at first it was just that, but then it became more. And now we're a family."

"I'm happy for you, but this isn't that. He refuses to tell me about himself."

"No offense Toni, but since when do you need to know a guy to get a few orgasms from him?"

A fair question, since I had no problem with the hit it and quit it lifestyle. "When a man goes so far out of his way to make sure he doesn't tell me anything about himself. It makes me suspicious, about him and his motives."

"That's something you'll have to figure out for yourself, Toni."

She was right, of course. "That's not at all helpful, you know."

Lucy laughed. "You want help? I say give him a chance, let him prove that he is or isn't worthy of you before you decide."

"You're terrible at this," I told her honestly. "It's not that simple Lucy."

"I never said it was simple or easy, did I? No, I did not. Nothing worth doing ever is."

A knock sounded at the door and it didn't take a genius to figure out who was on the other side. "Thanks for nothing, Luce."

She laughed. "My pleasure. Let me know what happens next!"

"Yeah, yeah," I groaned as I got off the bed and stood in front of the door, letting out a deep breath as I reached for the knob. "I'll think about it," I told Lucy before ending the call and tossing the phone on the bed. I inhaled deeply and exhaled as I squeezed the knob and twisted it. "Brady. What's up?"

Without a word he took a step forward and cupped my face in his hands, gently, despite the fierce look in his blue eyes. He stared at me like he wanted to say something and my gaze was riveted to the soft, unsure movement of his lips as if he couldn't quite find the words. A low grunt escaped and then his lips were on mine, soft to the touch but the kiss was hard and rough, commanding.

I submitted easier than I would have liked under his masterful kisses. They were all consuming and the swipe of his tongue so intoxicating that all I could do was hang on to him for dear life and hope I came out the other end unscathed.

Brady stepped forward, forcing me to step back again and again until the back of my legs were pressed against my bed.

And then I was falling.

In more ways than one.

Chapter 11

Brady

My hands and mouth were in absolute bliss as they roamed all over Toni's curvaceous body. My hands slid up and down her waist and hips, molding over every mouthwatering dip while I devoured her mouth, down her jaw and neck until I found that fluttering pulse in her throat. She was delicious in every fucking way, and the more I tasted her, the stronger my desire for her grew.

I pulled back and looked down at her with a heated smile as I removed her shirt. "I have a brown belt in Brazilian jiu-jitsu." My tongue slid back and forth over the swells of flesh above the cups of her bra.

Toni arched into me with a low, guttural moan.

I found the little clasp between her cleavage and flicked it open, revealing creamy tits and dark pink nipples. "When I read, it's usually historical mysteries, thrillers or biographies of historical figures."

"History buff," she moaned when I flicked my tongue over her hard nipple. "Hot."

I smiled and gave her other nipple the same treatment, losing myself in the feel of her silky soft skin, the sweet taste of her and the sensual floral scent emanating from her heated flesh. "Tacos are my favorite food, but any type of pasta will do in a pinch," I told her as I kissed the area between her breasts and then down her belly.

"Yes," she moaned when my tongue dipped into her belly button.

"My birthday is the first day of Spring," I revealed as I unfastened her jeans and tugged slowly on the zipper. "Lace is my new favorite fabric," I growled when my gaze landed on pale pink lace panties. I yanked off her pants, a move that forced my body off of hers, and tossed them behind me. "Beautiful."

"Fire sign," she growled and turned onto her belly, revealing that the pale pink was a thong. "Unexpected."

I leaned forward and sank my teeth into one fleshy cheek of her ass, which pulled a hiss from her lush mouth. I kneaded and massaged her ass as I kissed her from her lower back all the way up to her neck, pressing my body against her soft curves. "Hawaii is my favorite vacation spot." I moved her hair aside and nibbled my way from her neck to her shoulder.

Toni arched against my aching cock, rubbing her ass against me until my vision blurred. "Luau fetish?"

I laughed and kissed her other shoulder. "Surfing."

"Another surprise," she moaned and I was met with a

gorgeous smile when I turned her onto her back. Her fingers tangled in the hem of my shirt and pulled it over my head.

I smiled, kissing the spot just above her pink thong. "I've been jacking off to thoughts of you since you showed up," I admitted before I slid lower, pushing her thighs open with my shoulders.

"What was I doing?" Toni sat up on her elbows and smiled at me.

"What weren't you doing," I shot back and hooked my finger through her panties, sliding my tongue between glistening wet folds.

"Oh. Fuck." She moaned loudly and her head fell back. Her hips swirled, hungry to get closer to my mouth. "Yes, Brady."

I smiled against her and then sucked her clit until she began to vibrate. "You took my cock in your mouth," I growled swiped my tongue from her opening to her clit. "Took it deep until you choked."

"Oh fuck, will I choke?" She asked through harsh, breathless pants.

I laughed at the question just as I slipped my tongue into her pussy, fucking her slowly as she writhed beneath me and gripped my hair tight enough to sting. "You will," I promised softly, forcing her eyes to meet mine. "Would you like that, Toni? You want me to fuck that sassy mouth of yours?"

She nodded, her lips parted into a lusty expression. "Maybe you'll find out. If you're good."

"I'll show you good," I told her and gripped her thighs while I devoured her, lapped up her juices as she shook and quivered under my tongue.

"Brady," she cried, hips grinding against my mouth.

I moaned against her when she wrapped her legs around me, hips bucking up meeting every swipe of my tongue. Her pussy nectar was thick and sweet as it coated my tongue.

"Oh, Brady!" Her hips moved in a steady rhythm but I wanted her to lose control.

I needed her to. "Don't come yet," I commanded as I slid one and then two fingers deep into her wet heat, plunging in quick, shallow thrusts.

"Tease," she laughed and the sound was sensual and throaty, fun.

"That's another thing about me, I like to be in control Antonia." I added a third finger to the mix, flicking my tongue at a furious pace against her clit and I couldn't look away from the blissed out expression on her face. Full lips tipped into a teasing smile like she knew a joke no one else was privy to as her body trembled with the need to come.

"Brady," she growled. "Payback is a bitch."

I laughed against her, the vibrations pulling her orgasm closer to the surface, inch by inch. She was so close. I pulled back and blew gently on her clit. "Payback can be fun. Not yet," I told her and curled my tongue around her clit again and again.

"We'll see," she moaned and arched into my mouth. "Brady," she growled.

I increased my speed, pumping in long, powerful strokes as I flatted my tongue and teased her clit mercilessly. "Now," I ordered against her and less than a second later, Toni came apart. She shook and trembled through her orgasm, coating my tongue in her pleasure. Her fingers tightened in my hair and I didn't give a damn if she left a bald spot, because the sound of her, the taste of her orgasm, was pure perfection.

"Holy fuck, Brady." She smiled and collapsed against the bed, breathing hard and laughing. "Dirty, dirty boy."

I laughed and kissed my way up her body, my fingers still buried in her still pulsing pussy. "Me? I'm just a simple guy. A bit on the nerdy side, but everyone has their thing."

"Nerdy?" She laughed. "Sure. Simple? Anything but." Her eyes widened and then went dark with lust when I pulled my fingers out of her body and licked them clean one by one. "Dirty. Sexy. Nerdy." She pushed at my chest and straddled my body, grinding against my denim covered erection.

My hands went to her gorgeous tits, kneading them and tweaking her nipples. "Is this payback?"

"No." She shook her head and kissed her way down my body, pulling off the rest of my clothes until I was completely naked and she could look her fill. "This is foreplay. Payback comes later."

I knew I was in trouble when she nibbled her way down my ribcage, drawing deep guttural sounds from me. When she flicked her tongue over my nipples and I growled my pleasure, I knew she meant business. Toni kissed her way back and forth across my chest and down to my hips, and even lower. She teased me all over until I begged for her, right where I wanted her. Where I needed her. Where I throbbed for her. "Toni."

She smiled up at me, placing open mouthed kisses on my hip bones as her tits brushed across my erection. She giggled at the way my body vibrated and trembled with need before she finally gripped my length in her hand, flicking her tongue over the bead of liquid at the tip and humming her pleasure. "He's so pretty," she whispered, almost reverently.

I scoffed at her description, but before I say more, her lips wrapped around my cock and she took me so deep I thought she might swallow me whole. "Oh, fuck. Toni."

She laughed around me, the heat and moisture combined with the vibrations yanked my hips forward until I was so deep in her mouth I worried I really might choke her. Her eyes sparkled with heat and mischief when her tongue flicked out to my sac. Every time she got a reaction out of me, her eyes turned to molten lava and she pushed the limit.

After a while all I could do was lay there and watch as Toni took my cock deeper and deeper, pulling all sorts of erotic sounds from me as she gave me the greatest pleasure I'd ever known. She hummed her pleasure as if it was as much as my own, gripping me tight and taking me deep while she stroked me with capable hands. "Ah, fuck Toni!" My hips bucked up and she took me even deeper, swallowing around my tip. The sensation was so satisfying my eyes crossed and my body tensed with need.

"So responsive," she groaned before she took me deeper again and again, bringing to the point my feet were perched on the edge of everything before she eased off and started all over again.

"Toni," I growled in frustration.

She laughed. Isn't this your jerk off fantasy?" Before I could answer she leaned forward, grasping my cock between her fleshy tits and taking me in her mouth.

"Holy fuck!" It was the only phrase my brain could process as she overloaded my senses with her soft skin, her hot, wet mouth and those sensual growls as if she liked sucking me off as much as I liked being sucked off. "Toni," I growled, bucking forward at a fast pace as my hands tangled in her hair. "Oh fuck, Toni."

She didn't back off, instead she let me set the pace. She let me play out my fantasy until my sac tightened, my cock thickened and I pumped my release down her throat. She swallowed every drop before pulling back with a smile. "I knew you were a naughty boy."

Even after the orgasm, my cock was hard and aching, hungry to slip inside her body and hear those precious mewls again and again. "Your mouth is a work of fucking art."

She smiled. It was a shy, sweet smile that was so at odds with the ballsy woman I knew. "I'm glad you approve."

"Oh, I do," I growled and pulled her up so her body

was flush against mine before I rolled Toni onto her back, pressing my erection between her legs. "So much that I can hardly think."

"Thinking is overrated," she shot back and pushed her pussy against me. "Don't think Brady, just feel."

That's exactly what I did, let the feel of her guide me. She was so wet that I slid deep in with one long thrust, her low groan of pleasure telling me she liked the way I filled her. "So fucking tight," I groaned and took her mouth in a punishing kiss that left us both breathless and crazed with desire.

"Brady," she whispered in my ear, nipping the lobe as her hips swirled and she pulsed all around me. "You feel so good."

In response to her passionate words, I thickened inside of her. Her damp walls gripped me tight and all I could focus on was the pleasure that swamped my body. The layer of sweat that covered my flesh as she pulled me deeper and deeper, whispering dirty things in my ears. "Don't come, Toni."

She shook her head, nipping at my jaw line. "I'm gonna. You feel too good. Too thick and hard."

"Fuck," I grunted as she pulsed tighter and faster around me. It was too much to take and I pushed forward, surging deeper as I pressed my lips to hers. "Now," I whispered against her mouth and we flew apart together. Our bodies nothing but flailing limbs that jerked and shook as pleasure worked its way to the surface before it shot out of us both.

"Wow," she panted when her muscles loosened and she sank into the mattress beneath me. "That was super hot."

I laughed because I couldn't agree more. "It was," I growled and kissed her again, slow and hot. "And we're just getting started," I promised, holding her body to mine as I turned onto my back and we started the fire all over again.

It was the best sex of my life. The most fun I'd ever had with a woman, and by the time the sun rose, I knew that I would never, ever, get enough of Toni.

Chapter 12

Toni

The alarm sounded, jarring and obnoxious as it pulled me from the most delicious dream imaginable. Brady was naked with his strong, lean body wrapped around mine. He kissed my sensitive skin and told me I was beautiful as his fingers, his mouth and his dick, did wickedly wonderful things to me. He yanked orgasm after orgasm from my body with just a flick of his wrist or his tongue.

I moaned and a set of masculine arms tensed around me. My eyes flew open, and for the fifth time in as many days, I came awake shocked by the fact that Brady was in my bed. Naked. Sleeping.

"You're thinking too hard again." His lips brushed a sensitive spot behind my ear and I shivered. Brady laughed. "Good morning, Antonia."

"Morning," I grumbled, secretly loving the way my full name sounded on his lips. My body instinctively relaxed against Brady's hard chest with a sigh. My nipples beaded, and almost as if he could sense it, his big hands were there, grabbing my breasts and then pinching my nipples. "The morning is becoming better," I moaned.

Brady laughed. "That's better."

I rolled my eyes, thankful he couldn't see me. "It's seven," I told him the same way I had every morning this week.

"It's Friday," he shot back.

"Still a workday for some of us." I wasn't the boss here. Even though I didn't say it and neither did Brady, we both knew it was true.

He groaned and rolled me onto my back before settling his body against mine. "I have work to do too," he whispered, brushing a tantalizing kiss to my lips. "I just find you far more appealing than work."

I wanted to ask him what his work was exactly, but it would start another argument or another distracting round of sex. I preferred the latter, but it only reminded me of the former. "Lucky me," I purred sincerely. A man like Brady was a certified workaholic, I recognized it easily because I'd grown up with one, and the fact that I made him not want to work was flattering.

"Luckier me," he growled and pushed his morning erection between my thighs. We came together hard and fast, both of us reached that peak in just a few minutes, leaving less than five before the alarm clock sounded again, bursting the bubble and reminding us that it was back to the real world. "I need a week with you on a remote island. And no clothes."

I laughed and basked in his praise, and his post-coital kisses. "Sounds good to me." It was too bad he didn't trust me with the basic details of his life. *Forget it, Toni. Enjoy this, whatever it is, while it lasts.*

That's what I'd vowed to do, and just like every morning this week, I spent the time in the shower strengthening my resolve, ignoring my soft heart that wanted to make excuses for the secrets. The shield he kept between us. By the time I made my way downstairs, I was dressed to kill in black leather leggings, and a plain white lace t-shirt, I felt like a new woman.

Mostly.

"Good morning," I said to Layla in a sing-song voice.

She looked up from her tablet with a bright smile. "Good morning, Toni! What are we doing today?"

I froze because it was the first time in years I'd fallen down on the job. I hadn't planned any activities for her today because I was too busy getting in her guardian's—by boss's—pants.

"Um, I'm not sure," I said honestly. "I figured we could spend an hour or so drawing and then you can decide what you want to learn today. That will determine what our next activity will be."

Her eyes, so much like her uncle's, widened in surprise. "Me?"

I nodded as I poured a mug of coffee. "Yep. The best

way to keep learning is having a desire to learn so today it's dealer's choice. You pick what you want to know about and together we'll find a way to make it work."

"Cool!"

Heavy footsteps sounded and then Brady appeared, looking as if he'd just walked off the runway in a three-piece suit that made his dark hair and light eyes pop. The phrase *devastatingly handsome* came to mind instantly. Lust surged through me and when it faded, I frowned.

"Going somewhere fancy?" It looked like a date night outfit, except it was early in the morning, and he worked at home so it was...unusual.

Brady seemed shocked at my question and he looked down at his designer, bespoke suit and shrugged. "No. I have meetings that require my presence at the office."

The office.

It was such a bland statement, purposefully so, and everything in me wanted to push him, to ask who the meetings were with and if they were important to his business. But I didn't. He would frown and then freeze up, and ultimately ignore the questions altogether.

"Cool," I said in a chilly voice. "Have fun."

His brows furrowed in confusion, but as expected, he shrugged off the uneasiness and smoothed his hands down the beautiful fabric. "I don't know about fun," he offered. "But let's hope it will be productive and fruitful."

"Good luck?" What the hell else was I meant to offer other than that? This wasn't a normal relationship because it wasn't a relationship, it was a situation-ship, one where we didn't share personal details. Well, he didn't. I was an open book.

"Thanks," he murmured mostly to himself before he filled up a to go mug and left with hardly a goodbye to me or his niece.

"Uncle Brady is being weird," Layla declared without looking up from her tablet.

"Adults are sometimes weird," I offered diplomatically.

"You're being weird too." She frowned as she studied me a little too carefully.

"You're weird," I shot back with a teasing smile. "Drawing time starts in two minutes so we better get our supplies." Distraction was a nanny's best tool when it came to little girls who were far more perceptive than they should be.

We spent most of the day at a music shop where we practiced math skills and music with the guitar, piano, tambourine and the drums. It was a fund adventure, and by the end Layla had been absolutely enamored with the idea of playing an instrument.

"I'm going to learn to play three instruments," she declared as we left the shop. "Is that a thing?"

I nodded. "Sure is. I play piano and violin very well, the drums and guitar not grea,t but well enough to impress." My mother had insisted on the first two when I was about five years old and the other two came about as an act of teenage rebellion and self-discovery.

"I'll ask Uncle Brady." She beamed an excited smile and placed her hand in mine. "Look, Toni, ice cream!"

It was a gourmet ice cream shop where they made the flavors in house. "Let's get some for dessert."

She looked up with wide eyes. "And just a little for now? Please?" She pushed her bottom lip out and batted her eyelashes.

I laughed. "That might work on your uncle but I'm a professional."

She giggled sweetly, smiling triumphantly when the middle-aged woman behind the counter offered up several samples without checking that it was all right. "I love this place!"

"I'll bet," I mumbled as we made our way to the car and back to the mansion that was starting to feel a lot like home. My feet froze as we stepped inside. The house smelled like food. Warm and delicious, and flavorful food.

"Who's here?" Layla's voice was shaky and her hand tightened in mine, which was the first sign that the little girl was uneasy.

"Only one way to find out." I gave her a supportive squeeze and led the way towards the kitchen where Brady stood wearing an apron as he stood in front of the stove.

"Uncle Brady made dinner?" Layla's confusion was palpable and the hurt on her face was perplexing. "What's wrong?" She asked in a shrill, shaky voice.

Brady turned to his niece. "Nothing's wrong. I finished work early and figured it was my turn to cook. I made lasagna and bought salad, fried ravioli with three dipping sauces and tiramisu." He looked to me and then the little girl. "Layla what did I do?"

"Nothing," she said barely above a whisper and dropped my hand before she fled the kitchen for the safety of her bedroom.

"What did I do?" His silver blue eyes were wide and stricken, worried he might've done something to hurt Layla. "Toni?"

I sighed and shook my head. "It's not you, it's the situation. She thought you were going to give her bad news."

"What kind of bad news would I give her?"

I shrugged. "She lost her parents, Brady. That shakes a kid to their core and anything that comes close to that moment, it's emotional." The poor kid just needed a minute. "Her parents' housekeeper had watched her make her favorite snack, and then told her that her parents were dead and not coming back."

"I never cook," he sighed and rubbed a hand over his face.

"Yeah. She might've assumed, you know..." I said vaguely, because I didn't want to be the one to remind him of his behavior towards his niece.

"Assumed what?" he barked at me, his voice tight and angry.

"That you were gearing up to send her away," I said in a flat tone.

"Dammit," he growled and moved the sauce off the hot burner. "What more can I do?"

"This isn't about you, Brady. It's about Layla and her trauma. All you can do is be here and keep being here for her. Make her feel welcome and wanted and loved. Can you do that?"

"Of course I can."

I smiled at his indignation. "Then do that, and she'll come around." Unable to help myself, I crossed the kitchen to offer him a supportive shoulder squeeze. "She's emotional and she needs to process her feelings. Give her a few minutes."

His gaze shifted and darkened as his arms wrapped around my waist. "A few minutes, you say?"

My face flamed with heat and an unstoppable smile as I nodded.

"Thank you, Toni." His words came out on a low, and then his mouth was on mine, hungry and intense. He kissed me as if he missed me, as if we hadn't spent all night —for the past week—wrapped up in one another. It was the kind of kiss that made your toes curl, that made your heart pound so loudly you can't hear anything else.

Brady's kisses made me feel drunk and I clung to him as my legs weakened and my core tightened, my whole body flushed with heat. I moaned and he swallowed it, pulling me closer so not even a gust of wind could fit between us.

"Wow," I sighed when he pulled back. "You're welcome."

His laughter was deep and rich. It was such a welcome

sound and the warmth it produced in me sounded the warning bells deep in my mind. "Anytime, Toni. Anytime."

The bells got louder because when Brady smiled at me like that, I forgot all the reasons why this was a bad idea.

Chapter 13

Brady

"Are you sure this is the best way?" My brows arched in Toni's direction, skeptical that such a simple solution could fix the devastated expression on Layla's face. How long would it take to forget that look? To forget that she still thought this wasn't her home?

"I'm sure," she said with a devious smile, holding her phone out with one hand and the tub of ice cream in the other. "Get in here," she ordered and shoved the tub in my hand. "Now, smile," she ordered and removed the spoon from the tub, tapping the tip of my nose with the pink concoction. "Perfect."

"I didn't agree to that last part."

Toni looked at me and then burst out laughing. "It's called improvising. I'm sure as a businessman you do that on occasion."

I froze at her words. Did that mean she'd looked into

me? Had Toni done her own research to find out what I hadn't shared with her? She hadn't brought up the fact that she didn't know me again, so I incorrectly assumed that it was dropped for good, but that one statement had me reconsidering. Did she know who I was and what I was worth?

"I'm not much on improvising. A plan is always preferable."

Toni snorted in response and shook her head before she turned her attention to the phone as she typed a message for Layla. "Come down now and there might be some left for you. After dinner."

"How is taunting her going to make her want to come down?"

"It's not a taunt if I plan to eat the ice cream just to prove that I mean business." To punctuate her words, she swiped the ice cream from the tip of my nose and licked her finger.

My cock instantly hardened, and when Toni moaned it turned to aching and desire. The need to have this woman was with me constantly. I didn't know what it was about Toni but I couldn't get enough of her and I hadn't felt that way in a long time. *Don't question it, just go with it,* I told myself as my gaze heated and I hooked an arm around her waist. "Tease," I growled and pulled her body against mine. Chest to chest, hip to hip.

She laughed and the sound was low and sultry, shooting another dark streak of lust straight through my cock.

Need surged through me and my lips crashed against hers, hungrily devouring her mouth, the faintest hint of the strawberries and cream ice cream covered her tongue. My tongue explored her mouth as if this was our first kiss, her little moans made me hungrier for her and I switched our positions, pushing my body against hers so Toni could feel just how much I wanted her. Again. Right here.

The feel of her curves under my hands as they slid lower and gripped her ass, bringing her flush against my cock, pulled a moan from both of us. The taste of her lived in my dreams, the feel of her tits against my chest, the faintest thump of her heart against mine was almost more than I could take. "Toni," I whispered against her lips.

She moaned and arched her hips forward.

In the distance I vaguely heard a door open followed by the sound of little girl footsteps. Thankfully ice cream was on the line, and the sound of her voice pulled us both out of the fog of lust before she appeared.

"I'm coming, I'm coming! Don't eat my ice cream!"

I took a step back, my gaze fixed on Toni's kiss-swollen lips and then up to the *I told you so* expression on her face.

"Works every time," she whispered and stepped around me with the tub of ice cream in hand as if she'd been eating it and not kissing me senseless. "I guess there's some left after all," she said and shoved the tub back into the freezer.

"Toni," Layla whined. "You didn't."

She shrugged. "Does this mean you're ready for dinner?"

Layla nodded and I took that as my cue to get back to the stove and assembled the lasagna before putting it in the oven. Behind me, they chatted while setting the table. "Why do we have two forks?"

"Because one fork is for the salad and the other is for dinner." Toni's tone was patient and knowledgeable. "Since we're eating salad first, we put it closest to the plate."

It was another bit of information that reinforced my belief that Toni had come from some type of wealth or privilege, which intensified my guilt over shielding my true identity from her. *She could know this because she works around wealthy families,* the cynical part of my brain added.

I shook off thoughts of secrets and focused on the food and then on my dinner companions. We sat around the table laughing and talking like a real family. I hadn't thought about work since I left the office, which was a first for me. Not one thought of the game or fixing bugs or the marketing strategy invaded my mind, because it was so full of Toni and Layla.

Had it only been a few weeks ago that I thought I was content to live inside a near silent home while I worked through all the daylight hours? It felt like a lifetime ago.

"Layla, I want to talk to you for a minute."

Talking stopped and her eyes widened, but she nodded. "Okay, Uncle Brady. What's up?"

I smiled at the question. "I'm sorry that I haven't been as good a parent as I should have been since you arrived.

It's not that I don't want you here, because I do. We're family and I love you, but I'm not used to having other people around and I'm not used to having to think about other people needing to eat and all that stuff. But I'm going to do better, I promise. You deserve that. And most of all, I *want* to take care of you."

She stared at me for a long time and I would've given up millions just to know what she was thinking. Her eyes, just like mine and her mother's, studied my face. "I believe you, Uncle Brady. And I love you too."

"Good," I smiled. "Now eat your salad."

"Do I have to?" She asked with a cheeky smile.

"Yes," Toni and I said at the same time as laughter erupted around the table.

It felt good, the noise and the chaos and the laughter. For too long this place had been quiet and lifeless, and with the arrival of a fiery beauty, everything in my life had been turned upside down.

And I couldn't find it in myself to be upset about it.

Sure there were secrets between me and Toni that prevented us from becoming more than whatever we were right now, but that was a worry for another day.

Tonight, everything was perfect.

Just fucking perfect.

Chapter 14

Toni

It was late enough in the evening that Layla was already asleep, but early enough that I wasn't. Brady was holed up in his office doing his mystery work that he didn't want me to know about, so when the phone rang and Lucy's face lit up, I answered with a smile.

"Well, well, if it isn't Mrs. Rush who's forgotten the little people."

Lucy's laugh sounded down the line, putting a smile on my face. "You're hardly the little people, Toni. You've got more personality in your pinky finger than most of us have altogether. How's the new placement?"

I rolled my eyes with a heavy sigh. "It's great. Layla's a wonderful little girl. She's wicked smart, and she's so spunky she could've been me in an alternate universe."

Lucy shared my laughter. "That's great. And how are things with Mister Hot, Neryd and Mysterious?"

"Complicated." That was the simplest answer for a

situation that was anything but simple. "Very fucking complicated and not in the good, he makes me feel all torn up inside kind of way either. Just plain complicated."

Lucy laughed again. "Does he make you feel all torn up inside?"

Yes. "Maybe."

"Liar," she shot back, her tone good-natured. "You slept together."

"Yes. A lot over the past few weeks." My bed still smelled like him, which only made me remember all the things we'd done together and to each other in the bed beneath me. But it also served as a reminder that we were always in my room, never his. Because behind his door were his secrets.

Lucy squealed with excitement. "That's a good sign. Isn't it?"

"No, Lucy. It's not good. It's terrible."

"Oh," she said, slightly deflated. "Is he that bad in bed?"

My head fell back and laughter exploded out of me because only Lucy, so in love with her hot, sexy husband, would sound so devastated by that fact.

"No, he's terrific in bed. It's the best sex I ever had, period."

"Okay, now I'm really confused. The sex is so good you've been banging nonstop and he hasn't fired you. What am I missing?"

"Everything, Lucy," I said dramatically. "We've been sleeping together. We live together and eat meals together, and we spend time together after Laya goes to bed. It all feels very intimate, like it's going somewhere, but it isn't."

"Why not?"

"Because he clearly doesn't trust me. I still don't know his last name or the name of the company he works for, or even if he owns the damn company! And that's not the worst part." I felt like a crazy person right now, overly emotional and paranoid, which was exactly why I'd stayed away from relationships these past few years. Men were more trouble than they were worth.

"What's the worst part, Toni?"

I looked over my shoulder and lowered my voice. "It's like he goes out of his way to make sure I don't know anything about him. When he talks about work he makes a point not to say the name of the company or offer up any details about his work. I only know its gaming, because Layla said something about it once, probably by accident."

"Maybe he's just not good at opening up?"

I appreciated Lucy's effort, but I shook my head despite the fact that she couldn't see me. "It's a trust issue I think."

"Trust takes time to build. Remember the rocky road Dante and I had to get to where we are today."

"Yeah, I know, but he's not even giving me a chance. He's already decided that I'm not someone he can trust with something as basic as his identity." Not just that, he's already decided that I'm clearly someone who chased after money and status, which meant he still didn't know me either. If that was the case, why was I so worried?

Lucy sighed. "Sometimes rich men are weird about people's motivations for getting close to them. You know that."

"Exactly! Despite the things I've shared with him, he still doesn't know me if he thinks that."

"It's a hard habit to break," she offered sympathetically. "Dante told me about the nannies who tried to seduce him. The women who looked at him with dollar signs in their eyes. It creates a complex, and I mean, who wouldn't want Dante with or without his millions?"

I laughed. "Spoken like a woman madly in love. Though I will concede your husband is smokin' hot."

"Right?" She laughed for a long moment before it died out. "But it definitely made it difficult for him to trust me. Remember when Alex came to visit?"

"The difference is that he was jealous, Lucy. He was jealous because he had feelings for you and worried you might be using him. Brady hasn't given me a chance." The truth of that statement rocked me. I sat up as realization dawned. "You know what? I'm not worried about it anymore. I can't be."

"What does that mean?"

"It means," I stood and paced the length of my room. "It means that I can't keep sleeping with him because he doesn't trust me or know me, and he doesn't want to."

"You have feelings for him, don't you?"

"No. Maybe. Hell, I don't know Lucy. But what I do know is that I can't engage in a risky relationship like that with a man who can fire me. It would be worth it if it was going somewhere, maybe, but since it's not, it definitely isn't worth it." I could find casual sex anywhere that wouldn't impact my career or my professional reputation. "You've been a big help this time, Lucy."

"Thanks, I think," she laughed just as the sound of a baby whimpering interrupted her. "Let me know how it goes," she said before ending the call abruptly.

Resolved, I continued to pace until I burned off the nervous energy that pulsed through my limbs. From this moment forward, Brady was just my boss. Our relationship was strictly professional. No more stolen kisses or late night talks. No more toe-curling sex.

No more earth tilting orgasms.

That saddened me, but it was what had to be done. I could get *just sex* anywhere, I didn't need to bring it to work with me. Sex was easy, but the connection we had wasn't as easy to find. Clearly Brady didn't feel the same way.

So, it was settled.

Chapter 15

Brady

"Can I buy you a drink, beautiful?" Once again I found Toni curled up on a lounger in the backyard, getting lost in a book.

She looked up at me, but her usually sparkling green eyes were dim, almost sad. "Just got one," she said and nodded to the martini on the table beside her, promptly returning to her book.

Okay. I took a seat at the edge of her lounger and placed a hand on her leg because I couldn't be that close to her without touching her. "What are you reading?"

"A book," she says softly. "About a decade's long search for a serial killer. Want to borrow it when I'm done?"

I frowned, unable to tell if she was joking or not. "Something's wrong." It didn't take a genius to figure it out. Toni was usually a straight shooter, a woman who didn't play games, but right now she wasn't herself.

She closed the decorative case on her e-reader and turned her gaze to me, and yeah, there it was. Sadness. Toni was sad. "Nothing is wrong, just clear."

"That sounds ominous." My heart lurched and my stomach flipped because I had a feeling that I wouldn't like whatever she had to say next.

"Not at all. I've been thinking, and we need to go back to our professional relationship. Only our professional relationship."

How could she say those words when my hand was still on her thigh and moving up. "What did I do?"

"Nothing," she insisted a little too harshly. "You're my boss."

"I've been your boss from the moment we met, Toni. Why is it a problem now?" It didn't make any sense.

"It's not a problem *now*, Brady. It's been a problem, but you're very good at distracting me away from the details of your life. I don't know you. I know very little about you."

"Not this again. You know me, Toni."

She shook her head and set her e-reader aside. "But I don't. There are things I know about you, facts that you might put on a dating app or an interview, but not you. And worse you don't know me, not if you don't trust me."

"I trust you with my niece, how much more trust do you need?"

She laughed, but the sound was hollow, almost lifeless. "You don't trust *me*. You haven't told me about you, your life or your business because you think I'm some gold digger out for your cash, and if you think that, you haven't been paying attention."

Shit. "That's not true." Was it? I trusted Toni implicitly. "I don't think that," I tried but it fell flat.

"It's something. If not, tell me something about you."

"What?" My heart raced and I waited for her to make her demands. She would ask about my business or maybe my net worth. Possibly the worth of my house, maybe the number of houses I owned around the world. Toni was different, but not that different. "Well?"

Her green gaze studied me as if she could read my mind. She scoffed and I stiffened, worried she just might be able to read it. "Your last name, Brady. What is it?"

Shit. Her question had caught me totally off guard, which it shouldn't have. She was right, I hadn't given her enough credit, hadn't truly listened.

She laughed bitterly, the smile that touched her face was disappointed. "Exactly. Let's just keep things professional, Brady. Good night." She grabbed her e-reader, finished off her drink and disappeared inside the house.

I was left totally fucking confused, a little hurt, and a whole lot pissed off, mostly at myself. Toni wasn't wrong, I hadn't given her the opportunity to prove she was different than the other women I'd come across in my life. I'd taken one look at her gender, and let's be honest, her circumstances, and decided she was like all the rest.

It didn't matter to me that the things she had revealed about her past said she was from a life of privilege, I'd still found her guilty of other women's sins. "Shit!" I needed to fix things, but to what end? Did Toni actually care about me, or did she just need to feel better about fucking her boss?

That was a shitty thing to think.

I shook off that thought immediately, recognizing it was completely unfair. She hadn't actually given off any signs that she cared at all about money, never mind *my* money. She hadn't asked for any gifts or trips, not even an expensive dinner. Really she hadn't asked for anything except details about me and my life.

I went to sleep that night resolved to do better by Toni. To give her the details she wanted, if that's what it took to keep her.

Toni, however, had other ideas.

The next morning she'd come down later than usual, long after Layla and I had finished our breakfast, and drank down a cup of coffee. "Good morning," she said to no one in particular but the words lacked her usual energy.

"Good morning, Toni!" Layla bounced in her seat.

That earned Layla a wide smile and small laugh. "Ready to get your science on today?"

Layla groaned. "No."

"Well you can't win everything," Toni said with a grin.

I waited for her to turn her gaze to me, to acknowledge my presence beyond the small nod she'd offered up, but she gave me nothing. "What kind of science?"

"Natural science," she offered in a bland voice. "We're going to the Museum of Natural Science."

"They have a great exhibit on King Tut," I offered inanely.

She nodded. "Thanks for the tip, we'll be sure to check it out." Toni finished her coffee and rinsed the mug before she disappeared from the kitchen without a word.

Layla turned furious eyes onto me. "What did you do?"

I blinked, taken aback by the vehemence in her words. "I didn't do anything. Why would you assume it's me?"

"Because I'm a delight," she said with all the hallmarks of a child repeating something she'd heard an adult say. "It must be you, Uncle Brady."

"I didn't do anything," I lied smoothly. "Maybe there's something going on in her personal life." Like the man she was sleeping with was an asshole.

Layla glared at me, stood and left the table without a word. She didn't even put her bowl in the sink.

Since both the females in my life were unhappy with me, I retired to my office and spent the day working. When dinnertime rolled around, I expected Toni or Layla to knock on my office door with a reminder but it didn't come.

I ended the workday just after nine in the evening and went in search of dinner, finding the kitchen pitch black and the whole house eerily quiet. Dinner was warming in the oven but there was no note, no hint of the consideration I'd grown used to over the past few weeks.

It hurt more that Toni wasn't blatantly rude, as if I wasn't worth her wrath, which was all kinds of fucked up.

She wasn't mean or angry, just aloof and quiet. Mostly she was sad and that made me feel like the worst kind of bastard.

I ate my dinner in solitude and vowed to do better tomorrow.

I seemed to be doing that a lot lately.

Chapter 16

Toni

"Stay for dinner, Toni. Please?" Layla did her adorable pouty face and it was downright irresistible, bouncing in her seat until I relented. "Pretty please?"

I rolled my eyes at her dramatics, but I couldn't deny that I'd missed having dinner with Layla over the past week. And the taco bar we'd done together looked too good to pass up. "Are you sure?"

"I'm sure!" She shouted back.

I was all too aware of Brady's eyes on me, so was my body, which damn near vibrated with a need that I was determined to shove down deep. My attraction to Brady could be managed easily, as long as we didn't spend any time alone together.

"Then I'll stay for dinner. You had me at tacos."

She flashed a satisfied smile and turned to her uncle. "Do you like tacos, Uncle Brady?"

"I love them," he answered with a genuine smile before his gaze swung to mine. "They're my absolute favorite."

As if I could forget one of the few truths he'd actually shared with me. I hadn't forgotten any of it, especially his flat out refusal to tell me anything personal last week and my subsequent retreat from our budding...whatever it was. For the past week—eight days to be exact—I'd kept a distance between us, both physical and emotional. It was better this way, no matter how much it caused an ache in my chest, no matter how awkward it was between us.

It had to be this way.

He'd made it this way.

"What did you ladies do today," he asked Layla, who was happy to fill in the silence with the obliviousness of a child.

She told him about what she'd learned during our lessons, which consisted of a lot of math in many different ways. Brady, for his part, listened with rapt attention, seemingly fascinated by the lesson plans. His gaze was genuine however, which only made him more attractive, dammit.

I ate my tacos, mostly in silence, letting uncle and niece bond the way they should have been doing all along. Maybe this was for the best. Maybe withdrawing from family time off the clock was promoting their growth as a family unit. Without me.

Maybe I should just do my job and stop worrying about the hot nerd paying my salary.

There was no maybe about it. This was the for the best, for all three of us. I let out a quiet sigh and enjoyed one last taco before I decided to call it a night. But Layla, the mischievous little minx, beat me to the punch.

"I'm tired now," she declared loudly. "Good night."

Brady stood, confused by the sudden end to dinner. "Mind if I help you get settled into bed?"

Layla looked so confused. "You want to?"

Brady looked adorable and vulnerable as he nodded his desire to help. "I do."

"Okay." Layla took his hand and practically dragged him out of the kitchen. "Good night, Toni!"

I smiled at the cheerfulness in Layla's voice, happy that she was finally feeling as if this was her home. When I was alone, the smile dropped and I decided to clear my mind by putting away the dishes and leftover food. The past week without Brady felt strange, which only highlighted how important it was to put some much needed distance between us.

We'd been sleeping together for just a few weeks, but sharing a bed every night and having most meals together made everything feel more intense in a shorter period of time. It was an accelerated non-relationship, and now that it was over, I felt heartbroken.

I missed him.

But like most emotions, I knew it would pass. Whatever I felt for Brady was genuine, but not sustainable because he refused to let it be anything close to that. So I would shove those feelings down deep until they faded to the point of nothingness. In the meantime I would maintain a healthy, professional distance between us.

And I would let whiskey be my assistant. Whiskey and moonlight on the terrace would be my salvation until I no longer needed it.

"Hey." His deep voice startled me out of my reverie.

"Hey," I shot back, my gaze focused on the stars that twinkled in the sky above.

"What are you up to?"

I bit back a smile at his attempt at small talk. "Star gazing." It was awkward as hell and I hated it, but this was how it had to be.

"Toni," he began and I braced for what I knew was coming. "I'm sorry if I made you feel like you weren't important." He sighed and raked a hand through his hair as he dropped down on the lounger beside me.

I shook my head, finally letting my gaze settle on his beautiful face. "I don't need an apology, Brady. I never did."

"Then what do you need?"

"Nothing." I hated that he seemed hurt and confused by things, but he created this problem. "I wanted what happened between us as much as you did, and I'm not blaming you for that."

His brows knitted together. "But you *are* blaming me for something?"

"No," I sighed and took a long sip of whiskey. "I just think it's best for both of us if we go back to being nanny and employer."

He growled his frustration. "Why do you want to know me so badly?"

"I work for you, Brady. I can get "just sex" anywhere. And literally anywhere else will be less complicated than this," I motioned between us. "This will get messy going the way that it is. Hell, it's already messy and that probably means I'll end up looking for a new placement sooner rather than later."

"I already told you that I won't fire you." He was breathing heavily, his frustration breaking through the confusion.

"You say that now but what if we continue sleeping together? What if I develop feelings for you and I want even more than a few details about your life? What will you do?" He looked so confused I almost felt bad for him. Almost. "The horror on your face says it all, Brady."

"It's not horror, I'm just not sure where this is coming from."

I stared at him for a long time and smiled. "You really don't get it, do you?"

"No," he growled. "I don't."

A sad smile crossed my face. "You act like a woman hasn't ever just wanted to know you before." Which had to be bullshit because Brady was handsome and funny and smart.

He laughed bitterly. "It's not an act."

My heart broke for him, but I couldn't let him break my heart out of sympathy. "Then it's too bad for both of us, because that's all I wanted from you. Well that and your hot body." *And maybe your heart.* But that was definitely not on the table, and his behavior now helped me come to terms with that fact. Sure, it hurt like hell, but now that I understood, his actions at least made some sense.

"Toni," he groaned when I stood and walked away.

"It's all right, Brady. I get it now. We'll go back to the way things were before we kissed and everything will be fine." I hoped anyway, but Brady's next words stopped me dead in my tracks.

"And if I don't want that?"

I sighed and turned back to face him. "Well then you have the power to change it, in a variety of ways."

He grabbed my wrist and pulled me back to him, a look of absolute anguish in his eyes. "I haven't been able to stop thinking about you, Toni. I missed you."

I smiled. "I missed you too, Brady."

"Then what the fuck are we doing?" He growled, fixing his mouth over mine before I could formulate an answer.

My arms wrapped around him and I pressed my body against his, hungry for his heat and his touch. I knew I should have pulled back, extracted myself from this hot as sin kiss, but I couldn't. He tasted like every dream, every fantasy I ever had, and when he growled into my mouth and squeezed my ass cheeks, all I wanted was him.

Chapter 17

Brady

I don't know how long I'd been kissing Toni, but it felt as if an eternity had passed while I devoured her mouth. She didn't push me away. Instead, she pulled me closer and wrapped her arms around me, pressing those delectable curves into me as if she too couldn't get close enough.

My hands snaked down her back and grabbed two handfuls of ass, pulling her right up against my hard and aching cock. She gasped and I moaned, pulling her with me as I stepped backwards until I hit the lounger. "Toni," I moaned and pulled her on top of me, gripping her hips and sliding her back and forth along my cock.

"Yes," she gasped and tossed her head back, hands resting flat on my chest.

She was so fucking beautiful it hurt to look at her, surrounded by moonlight, heavy red waves looking wild and sexy as she ground against my cock.

Mine.

The word came immediately and I knew it was true. Toni's hips continued to grind against me and I couldn't take it. I needed more, so I flipped our positions and settled myself between her thighs.

"You feel so fucking good."

She smiled up at me and I felt my heart stutter to a stop before it kicked into overdrive, pounding loud and hard against my chest. There was something about Toni that just fired me up. I always wanted her, always wanted to see her smile and be the cause of that smile. She pulled me down and our lips locked together again, moaning into my mouth as she rolled her hips against my cock.

My hands moved frantically, undoing her button and zipper in my eagerness to touch her. To feel her damp heat against my fingers.

"Oh," she moaned against me and her hips bucked up when I made contact with her pussy.

"You're already wet for me," I growled as I pulled back and stared down at her. "So fucking wet." I kissed her mouth and then moved lower, down to her collarbone and neck, tasting every delicious inch of her.

"Oh!" She cried out into the quiet night air as two fingers plunged deep into her heat.

"Fuck, Toni. Your pussy is so tight." The whispered words had the desired effect and I look down, watching as she pumped her hips against my hand in search of relief.

"Brady," she whispered on a shaky breath, letting out a low groan when I stripped her out of her pants and underwear before plunging my fingers back into her. "Oh god. Fuck."

I smiled and nipped her earlobe before kissing my way down her neck and to her shoulder. "I've missed this," I whispered. "The feel of your pussy pulsing around my fingers and my cock. Come for me, Toni."

Her body shook and writhed with enjoyment and I knew she was close, but she was holding back, likely trying to prolong the pleasure of what she incorrectly thought was our last time.

I pressed my palm against her clit and rubbed roughly while I fucked her with my fingers and within seconds she was coming apart, gripping my wrist as she bucked against my fingers until every last drop of her first orgasm was wrung free. "That's better."

"Yeah," she agreed, the word a low hum deep in her throat.

I laughed as I kissed my way down her lush form, stopping to suck and nibble on her tits, a move I knew drove her to the edge of insanity. Toni cried out and gripped my hair as I suckled her nipples and tugged them between my teeth. Even though she just came, her hips rolled greedily against me and she moaned when my mouth left her tits and continued down her belly. "Mine."

She moaned again, but she said nothing, not until I spread her legs wide and stared at her glistening pink pussy, pulsing with need. "Brady," she growled when I blew a cool breath against her hot pussy.

"God, I've missed this." My tongue slid up her

opening and swirled around her clit in a slow, drugging motion that tore a guttural moan from deep within her.

"Brady," she moaned louder as I gripped her ass and tossed her legs over my shoulders. "Holy fuck," she moaned and panted as I sucked her clit over and over, the overwhelming sensation making her hips buck against me.

I smiled against her pussy as my hands found her big tits, massaging and kneading them. The move pushed her legs tighter around me which was perfect, because I was surrounded by Toni. She was everywhere, nearly smothering me as I licked and sucked her clit in turns, loving the way she vibrated with pleasure and gripped my head, fucking my tongue while she begged for more.

"Brady," she warned, but it was unnecessary. I was perfectly attuned to her pleasure and I knew when her breath hitched that she was close.

My thumb and forefinger found the hard tips of her nipples and pressed hard as I slurped her clit as fast as I could.

Her hips bucked up and then down, she uttered a low, almost feral growl as she came. "Ohmygod! Ohmygod! Yes! Fuck, *yesyesyes!*" Her body shook and jerked as the orgasm tore out of her and I licked and sucked until she stopped moving. "Brady," she squealed and tried to push me away but I wasn't ready to let her go. She moaned when another aftershock rocked through her.

I pulled back and smiled at her. "Nectar from a goddess," I said and licked my lips.

"Fuck me, Brady. Please. Now."

In seconds my clothes were in a pile on the grass beside hers. I knelt between her legs, stroking my cock in long, rough moves to keep from losing my shit too soon. "Say it again."

"Fuck me right now Brady. Oh!" Her head fell back and her eyes fluttered shut when I entered her hot pulsing pussy in one quick thrust.

"You feel so fucking good," I growled. Her pussy clenched around me in tight flutters telling me she was close to her third orgasm. "So tight and wet for me." My hips rock faster and thrust deeper, hitting that spot that made Toni release incoherent sounds. "Ah, fuck, Toni."

The heels of her feet dug into my lower back and she reared up, met me stroke for stroke. Hard and fast we attacked each other, coming together ferociously, too hungry to think straight, to see anything but Toni. "Brady," she moaned, her head thrashed back and forth, her hands scratched at my chest.

My hands find her gorgeous tits again, squeezing and teasing them as I fucked her, hard and fast, the lounger screaming under our weight. "I can feel how close you are, Toni. Your pussy is soaked."

"Yeah," she panted. "What are you gonna do about it?"

I smiled, liking this playful side of her after being without her for so long. "Not much," I grunted. "Just make you come all over my cock." I pulled my hips back slowly and slammed hard and deep.

"Close," she moaned.

"Even wetter now," I smiled and did it again, pulling out slower and I slammed even harder and deeper.

Toni's breath hitched. "Closer," she said around a smile and a moan.

I leaned forward and captured one nipple with between my lips, sucking and biting while my other hand slid down her belly to her clit, using my thumb in a rapid back and forth motion that had her clenching hard around my cock.

She cried out and I sucked her nipple harder, fucked her deeper. "*Oh, yesyesyes! Yes!*" She came again, a rush of liquid between us only intensified the sensation between her walls and my cock.

My hips pumped, knowing I made her come so hard made my hips piston faster and faster until my cock erupted inside of her. "Toni, fuck!" My body shook and trembled until she carried every drop of my pleasure, and then I collapsed on top of her.

Toni's hands danced up and down my spine for several long moments as we both struggled to breathe. Her touch was both soothing and arousing, and my cock twitched inside of her. "That was...I've never done that before," she admitted quietly.

I laughed in her ear and nipped the lobe. "I've never made anyone do that either," I admitted. "It was hot as fuck and I'll remember that look for the rest of my life." She pulsed around me and I groaned.

"Incredible," she sighed.

I rolled off her and held her in my arms. "Fucking

amazing." I got to my feet and hauled her onto hers. "Let's take the next round upstairs."

A sad smile flashed and Toni shook her head. "I think we should sleep alone in our respective beds. Good night." She pressed her body against mine, wrapped her arms around me and kissed me so deep and so sweetly, I was instantly hard again.

"Toni."

She shook her head and backed away, not giving me her back until she disappeared into the kitchen.

I smiled to myself as I gathered up our clothes. Toni was right to be worried. This thing between us was much more than sex, and it grew every time we were together, naked or clothed. She meant something more to me and I meant something to her.

Which meant it was time to make her mine. For real.

For good.

Chapter 18

Toni

"Sleep well, sweet girl."

My body was stiff and aching as I bent to kiss Layla's forehead. The poor girl was dead on her feet from a long day at the water park, so beat she'd fallen asleep before we pulled out of the parking lot. It was a long and fun day, but the sun burned hot and bright which contributed to my own exhaustion. With Layla settled, I made my way to my bedroom with a plan to collapse into the bed and sleep until morning.

I stepped inside the room and closed the door, pressing my forehead against the door as I took a deep, cleansing breath. "Okay. Shower and then sleep." I toed off my shoes and turned, freezing in the middle of the room at the sight of a very large, very beautiful bouquet of flowers. I took a hesitant step forward, gasping in shock at the sight of the stargazer lilies with posies in shades of pink and purple, vibrant shades of yellow. They were gorgeous and I touched the petals reverently.

They were obviously from Brady, and though instinct told me to dump them in the trash, I couldn't bring myself to reject such a sweet gesture. My body hummed just thinking about last night with him, the way he played my body like an instrument he'd built for himself. The way he talked dirty to me, ratcheting up my arousal to unimaginable heights. It was more than I could take, I had to escape before I did something ridiculously stupid like tell him this was more than sex to me.

I fled the flesh and blood man but he invaded my dreams and turned them into fantasies of forever.

"Flowers almost as vibrant and lively as you. Yours, Brady Winsome."

I held the card to my chest as a giant smile bloomed on my face. He'd given me his last name. It wasn't everything, but it was something. He was trying and that's what mattered.

Is he trying, though? My brain just wouldn't quit, and reminded me that it was just a name, that Brady was giving me what I wanted but in such an insignificant way.

It was true, he was trying, but Lucy's words rang in my head about rich men being different. Brady was definitely different if he'd never had a woman who just wanted him for him, without the money and whatever status he held in society. That was sad, and he deserved so much more than that.

So I accepted the sweet gesture, smiling as I took my

time undressing and stepping into a hot shower where thoughts of Brady invaded my mind. Whatever was happening between us had the potential to be incredibly amazing, but history also told me it could devastate me, and I knew I wasn't prepared for that.

The truth was, I wasn't at all prepared for Brady. Most of the fathers I work for—single or married—I simply tolerated as much as one tolerates any unlikable co-worker. I ignored their looks and suggestive comments, pretended they weren't failing their children in pursuit of wealth, and I gave their little ones all the things they deserved from childhood. My feelings for him shocked me, and I wasn't ready to acknowledge them yet, so I focused on the earth-shattering sex. The multiple orgasms.

His secrets made that easier. And harder.

"Ugh, now I'm getting on my own damn nerves." I stepped from the shower and wrapped a towel around my body while I dried my hair with another. I wanted Brady. The flowers and the last name meant he wanted me enough—cared enough—to try.

That was enough for now.

I smiled to myself as went in search of my phone. *"You deserve a reward,"* I said and tapped out a quick text message. *"Thank you for the lovely flowers, Mr. Winsome."*

Brady responded immediately. *"I'd love to hear you call me that in person."*

My skin flushed hot at his words. *"If you can find me, you just might get your wish."* I laughed to myself and opened my underwear drawer, finding a few silky and lacy things to light Brady's fire, but none of them were right. Instead I spritzed some perfume on my pulse points and wrapped my body in a fresh towel.

And then I waited for Brady.

Ten minutes later a knock sounded on the door and I smiled. "Come in."

Brady stepped inside and his jaw dropped at the sight of me in nothing but a towel. "Antonia," he rubbed a hand over his jaw.

"That's me, Mr. Winsome."

He stepped inside the room, kicking the door shut before he locked it, his gaze never leaving me. "Take off the towel."

I flashed a teasing smile and shook my head.

"Toni." My name came out on a rough growl and I licked my lips at the heat that burned his blue gaze, the fire that had his cock surging behind his zipper.

"Make me." I wanted to tease him, to make him lose control. I needed to see just how badly he wanted me. Maybe it was sick or even twisted, I didn't care. I just needed to see evidence that he was in this the same as I was.

Brady stalked over to me and with a quick flick of his wrists, the towel fell to the floor in a pool of soft, thick terrycloth. "Much better." His lips tugged into a tortured smile as his gaze raked over me.

I trembled at the heat in his gaze, the fire that pulsed through his veins. His chest heaved in long, heavy breaths as his gaze raked over my body. I couldn't look away from the way his gaze consumed me, ate me up like I was his last meal, like I was the last thing he wanted to see. It was intoxicating and I stood a little taller, shivering at the way my nipples beaded.

"Toni, you're so fucking beautiful."

From any other man I would have said those words were lip-service, nothing more than seduction to make me succumb to his wants and needs. But the thready tone in Brady's voice, the way his hands trembled as he reached out to me, paid true to his words.

His mouth touched my overheated flesh even before his hands, kissing a trail of fire over my body that had me shaking and trembling as I begged him for something more than butterfly kisses, more than the hint of his fiery touch. "Brady."

"That's right," he growled. "Remember who's touching you. Who's making you feel like this. Remember it."

As if I could ever forget the way he made me feel. I wasn't a sentimental type of woman who saw forever in small gestures, but the reverence in his touch, the worship of my body as he placed his lips everywhere—my hips, my ribs, the underside of my tits, my belly button—it was all too much.

Every touch and every taste was so intense that I couldn't keep one thought straight in my mind. Brady filled my mind as he kissed me from head to toe while I trembled beneath his touch. When his tongue slipped through my folds, my hips bucked up wildly, begging for more of Brady's tongue.

He lapped up my juices and I knew my next orgasm was imminent but it wasn't just the pleasure, it was the way he made me feel, like I was precious to him. Like I was someone he cherished and couldn't live without, and when his cock plunged deep into my body, I arched into him and I let go.

"Toni, you're mine. You are absolutely fucking perfect, and all mine."

I didn't reply to his words because I couldn't. What in the hell was I supposed to say to that? I didn't know, so I arched into him and locked my ankles around his back as his cock invaded my core in the most delicious way. He kept up a punishing pace that made me feel like a woman who was truly desired for who she was, and not just what she was willing to give. To do. "Brady," I whispered in his ear and nibbled the tendons between his neck and shoulder.

He trembled and pulled back, his serious gaze looked straight to the heart of me before his mouth devoured mine, kissing me wildly and frantically, as if the world would end if he didn't taste me. I felt the same way as I arched into his every stroke, ran my fingers through his hair and pulled me closer and closer because I just couldn't get enough of him. He reared back and gripped the inside of my thighs, pounding into me like a man possessed.

Pleasure erupted throughout me, greater and more

intense than anything I'd ever experienced, and I was powerless to do anything but lean into the sensations as my body shook and convulsed violently through the orgasm. The force of the pleasure knocked my head back and forced my hips into a quick motion that sent him deeper. *"Oh. My. God."*

"Fucking gorgeous," he growled and pumped me quickly, deeper, until another orgasm burst out of me. "Mine," he grunted and pumped harder and harder until the warmth of his come filled my pussy and our bodies went completely slack together.

His silver-blue gaze seared into mine, saying more without words than he'd ever be comfortable saying out loud and my eyes fluttered shut. I knew that whatever existed between us was real, and it was scary as heck.

But I also knew that there was no turning back, even if there was, I was a hard-headed woman, determined to see this through to the bitter, terrifying end.

Chapter 19

Brady

I told Toni my last name and the world didn't crumble around me. I told Toni something important about me and so far, nothing had changed.

Oh, things *had* changed, but nothing world ending. She'd opened up to me, she'd given me everything I wanted and needed, and she hadn't asked for anything in return. She didn't suddenly find herself in need of designer clothes or expensive jewelry, she didn't just remember a sick family member in need of an expensive surgery. Toni was the same sexy, sassy woman that she'd always been, and that was a woman I couldn't get enough of.

Now that I had her again, in my heart and bed, a switch had flipped inside. I was more focused than ever on work, more productive than I'd been since Layla had come to live with me, and it was perfect. Everything was just fucking perfect. I worked late into the night after leaving

Toni with a satisfied smile on her face, fixing bugs and updating code until the game had finally started to resemble my creative vision.

The phone rang and I picked it up on the second ring. "Yes?"

Sierra laughed at my greeting. "Oh good," she sighed. "I was worried that aliens had taken over your body."

"Funny," I snorted at her good-natured ribbing. "You called for a reason other than to bust my balls?"

"Yes, actually. Just making sure that it was you who'd sent the teams all this work and not some hacker looking to steal our IP."

"It was me," I assured her easily. "Inspiration struck, and it couldn't have come at a better time."

"Inspiration?" Sierra laughed. "Is that what we're calling the smoking hot redhead nanny sleeping under your roof?"

"I don't know what you're referring to."

More laughter erupted down the phone and I covered my face. "Sure you don't." That was the bad part of working with certain people for too many years. It was hard to lie to them, and damn near impossible to keep the important details under wraps. "I'm glad you've found your inspiration, Brady. You deserve it."

I grumbled and shook my head. "Not so sure about that."

"Well I'm sure. As a woman who works in this business and who has known you for years, trust me when I say that Toni is nothing like the vultures out to trap you."

I believed her, mostly. But it wasn't that easy. "But how are you so certain?"

"Trust your instincts," she shot back easily. "If you're being honest with yourself boss, you already know the score."

I knew the truth, but I just couldn't let go. "Not sure that I do, Sierra, but I'm working on it."

"Good. That's all we can expect from any man. Good luck, I'll call if I have any questions."

"Okay," I answered, but the call was over before the words reached Sierra's ears. "Good talk," I said to nobody but myself and sighed, tossing my phone on the sofa across the room.

She was right about one thing, Toni was not a viper. She seemed to have no interest whatsoever in my wealth, but her desire to know more about me hadn't dissipated over the past few weeks. But her interest never veered towards money or even work, other than to know what drove me.

Thoughts of Toni had me hungry for a taste of her, so I got up from my desk and went through the house in search of my redheaded spitfire. "Antonia, where are you?" She wasn't in the kitchen or the living room with Layla.

"Hey Uncle Brady."

"Hey Lay, what're you up to?"

"I made you a picture!" Her proud smile was contagious, and I put my search for the nanny on hold, sitting beside my niece to compliment her artwork.

"What did you draw?" I peeked over her shoulder and

my mouth hung open. "Holy shi- crap, did you draw this for real?"

She looked up at me with a sparkle in her eyes. "Yeah, I did. What do you think?"

I was stunned into silence at her talent. "I think this is wonderful." The sketch was so lifelike it was jarring, the way she'd captured me deep in thought, my gaze staring off into space with a thoughtful expression. "This is incredible, Layla. I mean, you're seriously talented."

"Duh, Uncle Brady." She giggled, and the sound was wonderful and adorable. "You really like it?"

"No, I really *love* it. I've never seen a sketch so life-like before. How...why did you draw this?"

"Because I like to draw, and I wanted to draw you something."

"Well I love it, so I think you need to tell me the best way to hang it. Should I buy a frame or can I just nail it to the wall."

Layla shrugged, laughing sweetly. "I don't know, Uncle Brady, I'm seven."

"Oh now you're *only seven*? Any other time you're the most mature seven year old on the planet, but now when I need your help, you play the kid card."

"You're funny," she said and erupted into a fit of giggles.

"I love it, Layla. Thank you." I did something I'd never done before, I wrapped my arms around my niece and smacked a loud kiss against her cheek. "Thanks."

Her cheeks flushed an adorable shade of pink and I

gave her one last squeeze before I went in search of Toni. My fingers itched to touch her, my mouth vibrated with the need to taste her succulent lips. My heart raced to set eyes on her again.

"Looking for someone?" Toni called out to me and I turned to face her with a smile.

"Holy fuck, Toni." She wore a simple outfit of skintight jeans and a white tank top that molded over all of her curves. Her nipples were hard and her mouth was slightly open. "You're gorgeous."

She smiled. "You were looking for me, Mr. Winsome?"

I nodded. "I was. Are you busy?"

"Nope. What's up?" She grinned again and leaned against the wall, arching her back, which drew my eyes to her beautiful breasts.

"I'd like to take you out. On a date." Where in the hell those words came from, I had no idea.

"A date?" She nearly choked on the word, which wasn't the reaction I was hoping for. "Seriously?"

I nodded. "Is that something you'd like to do?" I felt nervous for some reason and I tried to shrug the feeling off.

"Yeah," she grinned. "Of course. That sounds lovely."

"Where would you like to go?"

Her green eyes widened and she licked her lips. "I know the perfect place!"

My heart lurched at her words, but I swallowed down the worry and smiled. "Sounds good." I hadn't planned a date in years, and even if she chose the most expensive restaurant in the state, I would be all right with it. "Are you nervous about taking me out, Brady?"

"Yes," I growled. "Incredibly nervous. You?"

"A little, but I'm also excited. I'm curious to see what 'Date Brady' is like."

"Date Brady? Is he supposed to be different from regular, everyday Brady?"

"I don't know," she shrugged. "That's why I'm curious to see for myself. When?"

"Tomorrow? I can arrange childcare for Layla, I'm sure." I hoped.

Toni tossed her head back and laughed. "I'll take care of it, handsome. No worries." She cupped my cheek and leaned in gently until we were chest to chest and brushed her lush lips against mine. "See you tomorrow," she purred and walked away.

"We still have dinner at home tonight."

She laughed and waved at me over her shoulder. "I think we could use a little a few hours apart. It'll make tomorrow even more fun, don't you think?"

I laughed and watched the swing of her hips as she walked further away from me. "Wear those jeans again, please."

Toni stopped and turned with a gleam in her eyes. "I'll think about it."

I'm in so much fucking trouble, and all I want to do is run headlong into it.

Chapter 20

Toni

I tried on the jeans I wore yesterday one final time and smiled at my reflection in the mirror, because yeah, they made my ass look fantastic and gave my thighs a thick but slim look. But jeans on my first date with Brady? It didn't feel right.

I needed something hotter. Something sexier. Something that would make him swallow his tongue even before we made it to the meal. My choices were either leather pants which were sure to drive him wild, or a dress which would make me feel sexy *and* would drive him wild.

I pulled out the sexy deep green dress I bought a few months ago but hadn't found an opportunity to wear.

Until tonight.

The dress was sleeveless and velvet, perfect for the transition between daytime warmth and early evening cool. It skimmed my thighs so I decided to leave plenty of skin on display with a pair of strappy black wedges that would give me some height and even more swing in my hips. "Perfect." I felt sexy and trendy and most of all, I felt like myself.

There was no pretending to be someone else tonight. Brady would get the full unvarnished Toni, and I could only hope he liked what he saw.

I was a little overdressed for where I planned to take him for dinner, but that was all right. One thing my mother and I always agreed on? You could never overdress for any occasion. I touched up my makeup, finishing the look with bright red lips and lash enhancing mascara before I felt I was ready for this date with Brady.

At five minutes before eight he knocked on my bedroom door and I sucked in a deep breath, letting it out slowly along with my nerves before I answered the door.

"Mr. Winsome, you look hot as hell."

His lips spread into a sexy, surprised grin. "Oh. Thank you." His gaze raked over me and heat bloomed between us. "And you look like I'll be spending the night imagining what you're wearing underneath that dress."

My head fell back and I laughed. Feeling naughty, I lifted the skirt of my dress up and gave him a quick glimpse of the black lace thong. "Nothing at all worth wondering about."

His nostrils flared and he took a step forward.

I stepped back and put my hands up to stop him. "Uh-uh, Brady. We have dinner first." I laughed again when his shoulders fell in disappointment.

"Right," he straightened and flashed a tight smile. "Dinner. Where're we going again?"

"That, my friend, is a surprise. I just hope you brought your appetite."

His hand landed on my lower back as he pressed his chest to my back, his next words were whispered in my ear. "Oh, my appetite is big and strong, Antonia. I could devour you whole right fucking now."

My breath hitched and when I looked at Brady over my shoulder, he winked at me. Who was this sexy playful beast and where was my workaholic boss? "Good to know," I purred. "I'll hold you to that. Later."

* * *

"You're kidding. This is where you want to eat tonight?" The look of disbelief on his face was comical.

I bit back a laugh. "What? Were you expecting a fancy steakhouse or seafood restaurant?"

"No," he said, a little too quickly.

"Liar." I bumped his shoulder and took his hand, leading him up to the little beachside dive bar that wasn't really a bar. With a thatched roof and a small building where you could place carryout orders, it was *barely* an establishment. "This place has, in my opinion, the best tacos in all of Texas. Come on, you'll see."

Brady gave my hand a quick squeeze and let me pull him to a table on the edge of the beach. Like a perfect gentleman, he helped me onto the high-backed stool and let his hand linger on my thigh. "This dress," he growled.

"Better than the jeans?"

His nostrils flared. "Nothing is better than those jeans, but this dress? Fantastic." He licked his lips and leaned in, brushing a kiss against my lips so hot that my core quivered. He took his seat beside me and smiled. "What's good here?" He asked just as the waitress appeared.

"The fish taco platter is amazing, at least that's what I hear, but I usually come here alone, so I haven't had a chance to sample it yet." I held my breath and waited for disgust or exasperation to cross his face, but Brady's smile widened.

"The fish taco platter sounds perfect. As long as it comes with lots of different sauces?"

"It does," I said at the same time as the waitress. "And even better? The margaritas come in big ass glasses." I smiled at the waitress. "Strawberry mango for me and watermelon lime for him." I turned to him, expecting to see a frown or some other sign of displeasure but there was just a hint of amusement and a small dollop of affection.

"Sounds good to me. Now I just have one question. Is this the kind of place that has fresh chips and salsa?"

The waitress smiled. "On the house," she said and disappeared.

Brady turned his full attention to me, a smile on his handsome face. "So, did I pass?"

"Pass what?"

"Your test." He leaned in close enough that I felt his warm breath on my face. "Bringing me to this taco stand for dinner?"

"Not a test, I'm just allowing you to see me. The real me."

He studied me for a long moment and then sat back and stared some more. "And this taco hut is the real you?"

I nodded. "It is, part of me anyway. Just because I grew up with access to money and everything that brings, doesn't mean that's who I am. I love fish tacos and margaritas as much as I love my Louboutin wedges," I told him and kicked my leg out to show off my shoes.

"If the tacos are as good as you look in those shoes, I totally get it." He brushed a fingertip up from my ankle up to the hem of my dress. "A nanny who loves tacos and designer shoes. Tell me more."

"I like kids. But I grew up surrounded by nannies and house staff who were all nice, but I was a job, you know? Other than the housekeeper, I was a duty to them. I wanted to give kids an adult who was interested in them and cared about their everyday lives. Someone who cares about what they have going on beyond how it makes their parents look."

"Sounds like a story?" He leaned in close and took my hand.

I rolled my eyes. "It's an age old story of a wealthy woman wanted to mold her daughter in her exact image. I balked and rebelled at every turn, and our relationship worsened with every act of rebellion." I hated to think about the shit my mother said to me over the years and the awful things I said in return. "Enough about me. Tell me about you and Marnie."

"We were close growing up despite the age difference. She was my best friend and my protector, but she left for college before I was ready. We were as close as we could be as adults, but she and her husband traveled for work and I was busy building my company."

"Your company," I said flatly. It didn't take a genius to figure out he owned his own business, but that was all I knew. "What exactly is it that you do, Brady?"

His eyes widened in surprise. "You haven't looked me up?"

I shrugged and looked away. "No. I like to get to know people for myself, not through the filter of other people. I want to know what you want me to know."

He looked uncomfortable, but I promised myself that I wouldn't get upset or hurt if he didn't want to share.

"I'm just curious how you spend your days when you're holed up in your office. What fires you up?"

He leaned forward with desire swimming in his eyes. "You."

I bit back the disappointment I felt and changed the subject just as our margaritas arrive. "To the best margaritas in Houston."

Conversation shifted to more mundane topics that didn't mean anything. Subjects like sports and music, things I wouldn't remember tomorrow or the next day. The highlight, other than the view of Brady, was the tacos.

The moonlit walk on the beach should have been romantic, and it was, kind of, but it was colored by Brady's reluctance to open up and share anything about himself.

It doesn't matter, I told myself over and over again. He didn't owe me the details of his life. He didn't owe me anything.

"Toni." Brady stopped in front of me, pulling me from my thoughts. "Are you okay?"

"Fine," I said a little too brightly, punctuating it with a too-bright smile. "Just got lost in thought for a second."

"What's on your mind?"

I sighed and turned to face the water, black except for the moonlight glittering off the waves. I could've given him my usual snark and a flippant answer about how we don't share intimate details about our thoughts and lives, but I didn't want to do that. It wasn't a bad thing that he was wary of people. I got it. So I turned back to him with a smile, wrapped my arms around him and pressed my lips to his.

Brady responded instantly, his hands gripped my waist before sliding down to cup my ass. He moaned like his hands belonged right there on my ass, squeezing and pulling me close enough to feel just how much he was enjoying this kiss.

My eyes fluttered shut and I gave myself over to the moment and to the kiss. I gave myself over to this man.

But only temporarily, my brain reminded me. Brady wasn't mine, not to keep anyway. So I would enjoy this—whatever it was—for as long as it lasted.

And I wouldn't, under any circumstances, give him my heart.

Chapter 21

Brady

"Want some company?" I found Toni in the kitchen after I got Layla settled for bed. She stood at the counter island with her back to me, giving me an excellent view of her small waist and round ass in her uniform of jeans and a fitted tee.

"Sure," she said without any emotion.

"What's going on Toni?" She'd been aloof since our date, our date which I thought was pretty wonderful. Toni was funny and smart, she had opinions on everything, and I just wanted to hear them whether I agreed or not. She read a lot and loved to travel even though her job make it next to impossible.

But since then, she'd been quiet. She pulled back as if she was no longer interested in getting to know me.

"Nothing's going on, just making a sandwich."

Of course, because she hadn't eaten with us for the last few days either. "You're upset."

She turned to me, sadness in her eyes. "I'm not upset. Why would I be upset?"

"I don't know, but you've been quiet and aloof. You've stopped eating with us and Layla has noticed."

"I told her that you two need time together to find your footing. I just work here, but you and Layla will be family forever. That time should be for you two. Just the two of you."

Just work here.

"Is that how you see it, you just work here?" My nostrils flared and anger coursed through my veins. I got in her personal space because I wanted her to feel as uncomfortable as I felt.

She nodded, her expression indignant. "I work here. And we sleep together. That's it. Right?"

"Back to this again?"

"No," she sighed. "I've given up on getting to know you, Brady. That's not what you want. Long ago I also gave up on forcing myself on people who don't want me. I'm sorry if you don't like it." She skirted around me, rinsed her plate and sat it in the sink with a frustrated sigh.

"Toni."

She didn't stop as she made her way out of the kitchen.

"Toni!" I called out again and then went after her. "Wait." I gripped her arm and spun her to face me. "I'm sorry."

"Don't be." Sadness swam in her eyes, but she was far too tough to show it. Instead, Toni arched a brow, a challenge replaced the sadness in her gaze.

She was so beautiful. Tough and vulnerable at the same time. Beautiful and sassy. "Toni," I growled and cupped her face, kissing her slowly. Deeply. She tasted like heaven and sunshine, like leather and lace. She tasted like everything I ever wanted in this world, and I poured it all into the kiss, hoping she understood.

Toni gave herself over to the kiss the same way she did on the beach, pressing those delicious curves against me while I devoured her mouth. She moaned and gripped my shirt in her fists, silently begging for more.

Here, like this, she was all mine, and I wanted to stay in the moment forever. I hurried her in my arms and in seconds we were in her room. Seconds later, I had her completely naked and laid out on her bed. "You're so sexy, Toni."

She said nothing, but her skin flushed prettily at the compliment.

My gaze lingered on her body. Her pale skin and dusty pink nipples, hard and calling for my mouth. Her red hair splayed across her pillow matched the strip just above where she was swollen and pink and glistening for me. "Fucking gorgeous," I growled at the sight of her before I settled between her thighs, grinding against the warm juncture between her thighs.

"Yes," she moaned when I wrapped my lips around one stiff nipple, rubbing the other between my thumb and forefinger. Every flick of my thumb made her tremble and gasp.

I kept my gaze on her and switched my position,

watching the way her gaze darkened when I swirled my tongue around and around her nipple until it was painfully tight.

"That's so good," she moaned and gripped my head between her hands, keeping me right where I was.

I took the hint, licking and sucking her nipple, flicking my tongue over the stiff peak until her hips rolled faster and faster against me.

"Brady," she said my name on a breathy whisper. "I need you. Now."

I don't know how I moved so fast, but I was off the bed, undressed and back on top of her in about two second, smiling as I stroked my cock and rubbed the tip against her swollen, damp folds. "Turn over. I want to see that sexy ass in the air while I fuck you."

Toni moved like a gymnast, twirling her legs around until she was magically on her hands and knees, back arched beautifully so I could see her lips, pink and bare and glistening from this angle. "Like this?"

I smacked her cheek and she groaned. "Just like this." I gripped the round globes of her ass and slid in, slowly at first but she was hot and wet and pulsing tight around every inch as I sank into her body. "Fuck. Nothing feels better," I growled and shoved my cock into her until I was balls deep. "Toni."

She arched a little more and pushed back, silently urging me to move. She clamped down hard when I smacked her ass again before she released a half-moan, half-gasp.

"You like that," I growled and give her other cheek the same treatment.

"I don't dislike it," she moaned when I pulled out and slammed in harder and deeper. "Yes." Her head fell forward as pleasure overwhelmed her, matching me stroke for stroke.

She was hungry for it, a stark contrast to her cool treatment earlier. I pushed those thoughts aside and pumped my hips harder and deeper, and when Toni dropped down to her elbows I slid even deeper until we were so connected there was no hint where one of us ended and the other began. "Toni. Fuck."

She started to move her hips in a way that grasped me tighter and tighter. My vision blurred and my sac tightened and I knew I was close. Too close. "Brady," she moaned when I reached around her waist and rubbed her swollen clit. "Brady!" She cried again, hips moving faster and faster until goosebumps popped up all over her skin, followed by a pink flush.

"Come for me, Toni. Come all over my cock. Now!" I demanded and I punctuated the word with a smack to her ample ass.

"Oh, Brady!" She tossed her head back, arched her back as her body froze while her orgasm worked its way to the surface. And then she exploded all around me, hot and wet as she pulsed and squeezed me, her hips still moving as I sank into her.

The force of her orgasm ripped mine loose before I could think about logistics like bracing myself. "Toni," I grunted in her ear as my hips pumped fast as hell and then slower and slower. "I think you broke my spine."

She laughed, the vibrations shot along the length of my cock as it poured into her. "You'll be all right," she said on a satisfied sigh.

I lay there on her like that for a long minute, inhaling her scent and relishing the feel of her soft, slick skin against my own. "It keeps getting better," I said, wonder in my voice.

"It does," she sighed and flipped on her back when I was finally able to roll off of her. "It's maddening."

My chest heaved and I turned to face her, resting my head in my hand. "Why?"

"Because you don't want any more than this, which means we won't always have this." She motioned between us before sitting up and looking around the room as if she didn't know where she was. "I need to get cleaned up."

I watched the way she walked so confidently to her private bathroom. "Toni?"

She looked over her shoulder, the light of the bathroom cast her in a golden glow. "Yeah?"

"I'm sorry I haven't opened up."

She nodded, but her gaze darted all around me, anywhere but on me, in fact. "It's all right Brady. You're not the first man who only wants me for sex." Toni flashed a sad smile and shook her head. "I'm a big girl and I wanted this too. I wanted you."

My brows rose. "Wanted? Past tense?"

She rolled her eyes. "Tonight. I wanted you tonight

just like this. I know what you want and don't want, and I still wanted you. Okay?"

I didn't know what to say to that so I just nodded. But when she closed the door behind her I couldn't help but feel like that was the wrong answer.

Worse, I was pretty fucking sure it was also a lie.

Chapter 22

Toni

I was an idiot.

That was the only excuse for why I continued to go against my better judgment and spend any time at all with Brady. Yeah, sure, he was gorgeous and nerdy, and so hot it set my panties on fire, but he was also aloof. Mistrustful, and even more cynical than I was. It wasn't a good combination for, well anything, really.

The worst part? I was developing feelings for my nerdy boss. He'd somehow snuck past my defenses without even trying, making me open up and feel things I thought I was long past feeling. He'd made me feel things when he refused to feel anything but orgasmic, which made the past week pretty damn tense.

And erotic because Brady was a revelation. The man was insatiable, sneaking up on me in the kitchen pantry for a quickie where he shoved down my pants, took me from behind while he left love bites all over the back of my neck and shoulders. He slipped into my room well after Layla had gone to sleep for the night and took me to the heights of ecstasy before we fell asleep in each other's arms. It was like a never ending dream sequence with fog around the edges of my vision and I was trapped into this beautiful time and place where nothing mattered but me and Brady. The things we did to each other and how we made one another feel.

It wasn't real but it was beautiful and kind of perfect.

A week of nonstop orgasms and pleasure was almost enough to make me forget that this wasn't building up to anything else. There was no obstacles to us being together other than the simple fact that it wasn't what Brady wanted. I couldn't change it and no matter how much I wanted to try—and I really fucking did—I knew it wouldn't change anything.

So I lived in limbo for more than a week. A sweet, beautiful limbo where I didn't think about the past or the future and simply lived in the present. I pretended that I didn't want more and that this wasn't going to blow up in my face spectacularly, and I just took what was given—and a little bit more—and wished it was exactly what I always wanted.

And in a way, it was. I was always a little different but when it came to my parents' social circle, I couldn't have been more different than my peers. Sure I liked a few designer brands but I was just as likely to pair them with thrift store finds. I didn't *care* about name brands so much as I indulged in what I liked regardless of cost, but with them it was all about one upmanship. And the guys? Well they weren't looking for a curvy loudmouth who had no desire to be molded into the perfect trophy wife, which left me to my own devices.

But that didn't stop me from dreaming about someone who saw me and saw beauty and authenticity. A man who saw that I was gruff and brash but also willing to help anyone in a bind whether it was backup in a fight, a pep talk or a kick in the ass. There was more to me than wild red hair, killer curves and leather pants. But so far, no one wanted more than getting into those leather pants.

Including Brady.

Since Layla had worn herself out at the park today, I took time for a call with Lucy. "Hey mama, are you free to talk?"

"Yes," she groaned loudly. "The kids are asleep and Dante is at work. The house is so quiet I think I might be dead."

I tossed my head back and laughed. "Well you're not dead but the peace sounds nice."

"It is." Lucy lowered her voice, a true testament to how coveted quiet was in a house with small children. "What's up?"

"Nothing. Just checking in with my girl."

"Baloney, Toni. Spill the beans."

"It's nothing," I assured her. "And even if it was *something*, it's nothing that neither of us needs to worry ourselves about."

Lucy let out a deep breath. "Well my life is diapers

and carpool and breastfeeding so you'll tell me everything and you will leave out no detail."

"Lucy," I groaned and covered my face with my free hand. "Let's talk about anything else. Please."

"No. You called me because you needed someone to talk to, so talk."

"You're not nice anymore," I grumbled.

Lucy laughed. "I'm perfectly nice but I'm also short on time so tell me everything and make it quick."

I nodded even though she couldn't see me but just as I did, the little minx switched to a video call. "Is this necessary?"

"Perfectly. Talk."

"Fine," Sharing my feelings wasn't really my forte but this was Lucy and she was the closest thing to a beat friend I had, so I sucked in a deep breath and let it out on a rushed breath as I told her the whole dirty story. "And that's pretty much it. He wants me but not enough to share anything personal with me."

"Brady Winsome," she said as if the name meant something to her. "You haven't looked him up?"

"No. if he doesn't want me to know then I don't want to know. Soon enough we'll go back to being nothing more than boss and employee and it won't matter who he is or what he does."

"Right, but you're not curious?"

"Oh, I am. But I'm also resigned. This is what it is and how it has to be, which means I'm working on being fine with it."

"You're hurt," she guessed correctly.

"Annoyed," I lied because it's what I did.

"Yeah, of course. That's what I said."

I chuckled. "You're such a good friend."

"I am, aren't I." Lucy sighed and shook her head. "You like him and if I had to guess I would say you *more* than like him. But your instincts are right. If he doesn't open up then what's really between you?"

"Really great sex," I answered. "Which isn't as important as I thought it would be. Holy shit, is this like growth or adulthood or some other scheme?"

"All of the above," she answered with an amused laugh. "Great sex is great but it's only great because your feelings are involved, so if they aren't returned or they come with strings, you might as well settle for emotionless really good sex."

"Damn. Have you always been this good at giving advice or is it marriage and non-stop orgasms, oh, wise one?"

"Um, all of the above?"

We shared a laugh and even though I didn't feel any better about my situation, just talking to Lucy made me feel better in general. "Thank you for taking time out of your busy new life for me."

"Always. And if you need to talk or a guest room to crash in, our door is always open."

"I appreciate that but maybe whenever whatever is going to happen, happens, I'll treat myself to a vacation I've been meaning to take for the past few years."

Lucy tossed her head back and laughed again. "Only you can say something like that and have it make total sense."

"It's a talent," I smiled and rolled my eyes.

"I'm here except for right now because I have to go. There's a baby in the house that needs to eat."

"Okay. Kiss your kiddies for me. Thanks again, Lucy."

"Anytime. Love you. Bye."

I ended the call and shoved my phone into my back pocket before putting away all thoughts of the future. For now I was determined—and yeah maybe a little delusional—to live firmly in the present.

Chapter 23

Brady

This is why I don't do relationships. Those words kicked around in my brain on and off all morning because my focus was divided, half on work and the other off stuck on Toni. Why was she the woman who'd gotten under my skin? What was it about that fiery red hair and sassy mouth that called to me and made me broke all of my rules?

Most of all, what was it about her that kept me longing for her even when she wasn't around, even when she didn't want a damn thing to do with me? *Like now.*

She's made herself scarce since she accused me of only wanting her for sex. *Just like all the others.* Her words had pissed me off but they'd also broken my heart just a little. How many idiots in her life had she encountered who didn't see how great she was? How sexy those curves were and how beautiful she was engulfed with passion? How did they not see what I saw?

Doesn't matter, does it? I see how great she is and I still managed to fuck it up.

"Dammit," I growled and shoved away all thoughts of Toni so I could focus on work. The teams were all caught up and some were even ahead of schedule and I wanted, no I *needed* to keep that momentum going. So I did what I always did when I didn't want to think about the world around me, put my head down and focused on one task at a time.

Sometime just after noon a sharp knock sounded on the door and I leaned back with a smile, knowing who was on the other side.

"Come in."

The door opened and there was Toni looking hot as hell in an unusually feminine dress, green with white polka dots and cut just low enough to give me a glimpse of her pale cleavage. "Hey." That one word came out shy, almost uncertain but it was at odds with her squared shoulders and straight spine, and the confidence that she oozed. "Busy?"

I glanced down at my desk and shook my head before returning my gaze to her delicious curves, the soft skin on display. "Not for you. No."

Toni rolled her eyes but I didn't miss the blush that crawled up her cleavage to her neck and landed in adorable dots on her cheeks. "Good." She stepped inside and closed the door, he gaze lingered on the papers for a second and then she looked away.

I pushed away from my desk, hungry to touch her now

that she was here. "What brings you by," I asked as I wrapped my arms around her waist and pulled her closer. The feel of her hips against mine, her tits against my chest, woke my cock up and I pulled back with a smile before my mouth crashed down over hers. Our tongues danced together but she let me lead and I devoured her mouth while my hands roamed every inch of her slender waist and round ass. My hips pushed forward and she pushed back, growling into my mouth.

Toni pulled back first with a dazed smile that I committed to memory. "Wow."

"You in that dress is giving me all kinds of ideas."

"Yeah?" She let her fingertips hang from my waistband and flashed a flirtatious smile. "Because you in those glasses is giving me a few ideas too." I didn't have to wait for an answer before she had my pants open and her hand inside my boxers, a strong grip on my cock. "All kinds of ideas."

My head fell back and a groan escaped. "I like this idea," I growled.

"Thought you might," she whispered in my ear before nipping the soft flesh at the lobe. A few rough tugs and the next thing I felt was my pants falling to my ankles. "Ready for me so soon," she purred.

I opened my eyes and looked down at Toni on her knees because it was a fucking sight to behold and not just because I could see straight down her dress. She kept her gaze on mine as she adjusted her hold on my cock, gripping me from the base before leaning forward to swipe her tongue across the beads of pre-cum with a moan. "Ah, fuck."

Her lips curl into a smile as though she liked my response and then my cock slowly disappeared, inch by inch into her hot, wet mouth. She hollowed out her cheeks and my cock was surrounded by heat and moisture.

I sucked in a breath and let it out slowly as she sucked me up and down, taking me deeper and deeper, swiping her tongue along my sac with every stroke. "Fuck, Toni." My eyes fought to close but I willed them to stay open, unwilling to miss one fucking moment of this encounter.

Her eyes sparkled with mischief as her lips scraped against me on the way back up and her grip tightened as she sucked the tip until my hips bucked. "Naughty," she growled and did it all over again, cupping my balls and taking my cock as if it was hers, as if she had the right. As if I was hers.

I swallowed hard as I tried to keep myself under control because with the way she was working me, chances were good that I might come far too soon. "So fucking good," I growl. "You like that?"

In response she squeezed my balls just enough to send another rush of desire through me. She hummed her own pleasure and that move brought me a little closer to the edge. She released my sac and one hand slipped around my thighs to grip my ass, urging me deeper.

I took the hint and slowly moved my hips to fuck her mouth. "Fuck, Toni. I can't hold back."

She took me deeper at those words and swallowed,

letting her throat circle my tip before she pulled all the back and swirled her tongue around the same sensitive area. "Who's asking you to hold back?"

A low growl escaped and I gripped a handful of red hair in one hand, tilting her back so I could watch her as I fed her my cock over and over, deeper and deeper until her eyes water but she doesn't let me slow down or stop, squeezing my ass as if to say *keep going.*

I thrust a little deeper and a lone tear slips from the corner of her eye but she doesn't let up. My grip tightens on her hair as my balls tighten and the base of my cock swelled. "Toni!" My body stilled and I exploded in her mouth and down her throat. "Fuck," I growled when she swallowed it around me. Every stream that escaped, she swallowed around me which prolonged my orgasm for an eternity. "Holy fucking shit," I grunted as the last drop hit her tongue and she pushed me down her throat one final time before she released me and my legs damn near buckled.

Toni licked her lips and stood with a smile. "Even better than I dreamed it."

My legs wobbled again and I leaned against my desk, hooking an arm around her waist. "You dreamed of sucking my cock?"

She nodded. "Here in your office just like that."

"That was...I never come so much from a blow job. Ever."

Toni laughed and the sound was magnificent. "Good to know."

"I don't know how I'll ever get any work done in here ever again." I would always see her in that dress on her knees, eyes fixed on me while she took my cock deep. The reminder of my work shifted my focus for a minute and I reached behind me to shut off my monitors.

Hurt flashed in her eyes when I turned back to Toni but she looked away too quickly for me to be sure. "Speaking of distraction, I came in here for a reason."

"Yeah," I pulled her close with one hand and slipped the other up her thighs and into her panties where she was wet and swollen. "Was this the reason?"

Her head fell back and her hips thrust against my touch. "No, but I'll take it."

I laughed and kissed her throat, pumping two fingers into her. "What is it, Toni. What was the reason?"

She swallowed hard and her pussy clenched tight around my fingers. "I need a favor."

My blood instantly ran cold. My fingers stopped and I slowly pulled them from her body. "A favor?"

She heard the shift in my tone and her eyes widened but undeterred, Toni nodded and folded her arms as she took a few steps back. "Yeah, Brady. A favor."

My brows dipped into a frown. "It was just a matter of time, wasn't it?" I needed some distance so I walked around my desk to have a barrier between us as my anger festered and grew. "What is that you want, Toni? A piece of must-have jewelry? A trip on my private jet? Those designer shoes you love so much? Lay it on me." I was an asshole and I knew it but Toni was just like all the rest. Oh sure, she'd hid it better and played the role to perfection but in the end it was all about what I could do for her.

"Are you serious right now?" She shook her head, her tone incredulous as if I was still that desperate nerd I used to be.

"Don't play coy now, tell me what you want. I'm feeling generous and you've more than earned it."

She sucked in a sharp breath and her nostrils flared.

Oh she was angry which was good, because I was angry too. "You have an investment opportunity you don't want me to miss out on? That was what the blow job was about, wasn't it?"

"No," she growled. "That was because I wanted to do it. I wanted to see you when I made you feel like that. But I guess treating me like shit makes you feel better."

I rolled my eyes, refusing to feel guilty when she was the one in the wrong. "Give it up, Toni. Just tell me what you want and I'll decide if you've earned it or not."

She took a step back as if I'd hit her but Toni was tough and her expression went completely blank, devoid of all emotion. She reached for the office door and turned the knob, tugging the door open slightly before her gaze met mine once again. "What I want from you, Mr. Winsome, is to keep an open mind when Layla finally works up the courage to ask you to buy her a guitar. She's getting good at it and she's excited to keep learning but she's worried you're going to say no. If you do, just think about it first." Her eyes grew suspiciously moist but she shook away the emotions that threatened to surface and walked out of my office, closing the door quietly behind her.

My heart pounded in my chest and I knew that for as long as I lived, I would never, ever forget that look on her face. I made her feel worse than shitty, worse than worthless like her parents. I made her feel like... "Fuck!"

I screwed up. Badly. Again.

This time I'm positive she will never forgive me.

I felt the loss instantly and my chest collapsed on itself. My focus went to shit for the rest of the day.

Chapter 24

Toni

Enough is enough, Toni. Get your shit together. I had the same pep talk with myself every morning for the past few days as I stared at puffy red eyes in the mirror, a sad expression and lifeless eyes. I cried a little, okay, I cried a lot for the first couple of days after Brady accused me of whoring myself out for gifts. I cried because once again I thought he was a nice guy who was scarred or wary after a few bad experiences.

Once again, I was wrong. He wasn't scarred, he was just an asshole.

Now that I knew who Brady really was—another rich prick—I could move on with my life. Today was Friday and I had the whole weekend ahead of me to wipe away all traces of the hot nerdy asshole.

As soon as Brady walked in the door, I hugged Layla goodbye and made her promise to be a good girl for her uncle and then I went to my apartment where I enjoyed a body scrub and then a long, hot bath. I scrubbed my skin raw to remove the scent of him from my flesh. I rubbed until I could no longer feel his hands on my body.

Two hours later I felt clean and refreshed and ready to be out amongst the people, but not exactly on a solo mission tonight so I picked up my phone and called a friend. "Molly, hey. It's Toni. You up for drinks tonight? On me?"

She let out a heavy sigh followed by a harsh laugh. "Well I guess that does sound better than peanut butter and jelly sandwiches and Netflix on my cousin's sofa. When and where?"

An hour later Molly walked into The Happy Heifer looking as if her week was just as shitty as mine. I waved her down with one hand and poured a tall glass of beer for her. "Rough week?"

She nodded and accepted the beer with a tired smile. "You could say that. my employer's new girlfriend thinks my curves are too tempting and they let me go."

"Insecure bitch," I growled and flagged down the waiter for shots. "I'm sorry that happened, Mols."

She sighed and scrubbed a hand over her face. "It's fine, really. I mean, it pisses me off but it's not like this is the first time and it probably won't be the last."

"It's bullshit, you know that right?" I shook my head, so fucking sick of this stupid mentality. "Your body is gorgeous. Women go under the knife to get what you have naturally and having curves doesn't make you slutty or easy or any of that shit," I growled.

"I know but thank you for saying it out loud, Toni." Molly was a sweetheart, which normally would piss me off but just like Lucy it was so genuine it was hard to dislike her. "Why are *you* drinking tonight?"

I sighed and raised my shot high in the air, knocking it back without a toast. "I don't wanna talk about it but let's just say that men suck." Even saying that much about it just brought back all the things I was trying like hell *not* to think about. But the dark look on Brady's face when he spit those hateful words at me? Top five things I'll never forget. But tonight wasn't a night to think about it so I let out a heavy sigh and shook off my feelings. "Do you think I'm a difficult woman?"

Molly blinked in surprise as if she didn't want to answer but then she did something people rarely do, she thought about it before she answered. "No. I think you're great and I wish I had even half of your confidence and courage. People don't mess with you because you just *seem* like you'll kick their ass and that's enough. Most of the time I don't even know who I am."

I flagged down the waiter for more shots as Molly's words sank in. "Knowing who you are and being yourself isn't always everything it's cracked up to be. Don't get me wrong, I like myself just fine. No, scratch that, I love myself, but sometimes I wonder if I'm paying too heavy a price for being myself." It was something I never admitted out loud but often wondered about.

"Toni," Molly growled with more ferocity than I knew she was capable of. "The price of not being yourself and being miserable? That price is too high. I've twisted myself into knots and been who I was supposed to be and what did it get me? Nothing. At least you haven't given up yourself to still not be enough for other people."

"Yeah, I guess that's a good point too." I shook off the melancholy that threatened to turn me into a drunken, morose mess. "I'm happy to go shopping with you to help you find clothes that fit your body, your style and your personality."

She flashed a sweet smile I could never pull off and knocked back her second shot. "That would be great, Toni. Thanks."

I order a third round of shots and when they arrived, I raised my glass. "All right let's toast to being happy with who we are...once we figure it out."

Molly laughed and finished off her third shot with a frown. "Hot damn that stuff burns but it's also smooth."

"That's because it's top shelf tequila." We ate too much barbecue and drank too much beer and tequila, and two and a half hours later we stumbled out into the street, tipsy and laughing as we fell into a rideshare, our troubles seemed a million miles away.

For the moment anyway.

It didn't take long thought for thoughts of Brady and his careless words to invade my mind once again. Then again, maybe the words weren't careless. Maybe he meant every syllable he'd said, which only pissed me off more. *No more,* I promised myself when my eyelids finally started to grow heavy.

Sleep was near and I was counting on the booze to help me have a peaceful sleep that didn't include thoughts of the mysterious Brady Winsome.

The next morning I woke up early and made breakfast because it was the only day I could enjoy breakfast without seeing familiar silver-blue eyes that tried too hard to figure me out.

"You made breakfast?" Molly reached her hands high above her head, stretching and yawning while she moaned over breakfast.

"I did. Dig in. You still up for shopping today?"

"If you are, I'm game," she said uneasily which meant it was up to me to take control.

After breakfast we spent five hours updating Molly's wardrobe before we settled into a booth for late—but healthy—lunch to make up for last night's misery indulgence. "I'm tapping out, at least for today," I told her as a yawn cracked my jaw.

Molly laughed. "Oh, thank god! I thought you were going to suggest more stores."

"Hell no. I'm going home to sit on my ass and watch movies until I have to go back to work."

"Want some company?"

Did I? Being alone would only allow me to wallow in thoughts of Brady and that was the last thing I wanted. I liked my job. I loved being the one who got to spend time with Layla and show her the world, show her that she could be anybody she wanted. Which meant I needed to get over it.

Fast.

"You know what, Mols? I would love some company." It was too long since I had a proper girls' day since all of my girls are all loved up and having babies. This weekend was just what I needed. When Monday rolled around it would be like the past few weeks never even happened.

Fingers crossed.

Chapter 25

Brady

Monday morning had dawned bright and early because Toni hadn't come home on Sunday night the way she usually did, spiking my worry that she wouldn't come back at all. She'd arrived just as the alarm sounded to wake up Layla and get her ready for the day, which gave me hope that I could find a time to apologize and get us back on the right track.

But that hadn't happened. Toni had done a damn good job of ignoring me all week. She orchestrated it so that she and I were never alone together. At mealtime it was just me and Layla, which was nice but I still missed having her close, and when she entered a room that I was in, she turned on her heels and left.

She didn't even pretend she wasn't doing it and I deserved it, and more. I haven't spoken a word to her in a week because she would give me a barely audible *good morning* and rush off before I could say the words in reply.

She spent evenings alone in her room and I didn't even know if she snuck down later to have something to eat.

It was maddening. Dammit, it was frustrating as hell that she'd so effectively cut me off. I deserved it, that was without question, but that didn't make it hurt any less.

It wasn't just the look she'd leveled me with when she left my office that I couldn't stop thinking about, it was the expression she wore when she told me I wasn't the first man who only wanted her for sex. Did she really think that I saw her like that? Like she was some sort of curvy fetish to try out and cast aside? "Shit," I growled and shook my head as those two scenes played over and over in my head.

Layla gasped. "You said a bad word."

"I know," I sighed and offered up a sheepish smile. "I meant it but I'm sorry you had to hear it."

She shrugged. "Mom and Dad said bad words all the time but Mom said I couldn't say them until I turned sixteen." Her silver-blue eyes took on a faraway expression for a minute before she dropped it and replaced it with a frown. "Did I do something to make you mad, Uncle Brady?"

"Of course not, kiddo. You're the best." Toni's words came back to me and my jaw clenched. She was right. Again. "Look Layla, even when do make me mad and act like a brat, you're not going anywhere. Except maybe to your room. We're a family and that means we're stuck with each other even when you make me mad and even when I make you mad. Got it?"

"Yeah," she smiled. "I got it, Uncle Brady." She continued to smile as she returned to her dinner but her fingers twitched the way Marnie's used to when she was gearing up to ask for a favor.

A favor. I hated that fucking word. "Talk to me, kiddo. What's up?"

Layla nibbled her bottom lip and sighed. "I want to learn to play guitar. I'm already learning but it's time for me to have a guitar of my own."

I smiled at the way she said it, as if it was a direct quote from someone else. "You want guitar lessons too?"

Her eyes darted left and then right before she found her courage and sat taller, confident as she answered. "I do. I'll be good and eat all my veggies and whatever else I need to do."

"You don't need to do anything extra, Layla. All I ask is that you give lessons a fair shot. If it gets too hard, don't just quit, okay?"

"I won't. I promise."

"Then yes, we'll get you a guitar of your very own."

Her smile lit up spectacularly and in that moment she looked just like my sister. "Thank you, Uncle Brady! Thank you so much." She darted from her chair and ran around the table, slamming into me with a hug and a dozen kisses all over my face. "I love you and not just because you're getting me a guitar."

I laughed and hugged her back. "I love you too, Layla, and not just because you said you love me first."

She giggled and squeezed me a little tighter. "Toni said you loved me but you didn't know how to show it yet."

Toni. Was there anything the woman didn't do well? "She was right." Again.

After dinner, I settled Layla in bed with a story and cleaned the kitchen but none of it was enough to burn off the nervous energy that made sleep impossible. I couldn't stop thinking about Toni, wondering what she was doing and thinking. I wondered what she was feeling. Had she thought about me at all?

Did she miss me?

I knocked on her door quietly, leaning close but there was no answer. I frowned and even though it was a gross breach of privacy, I pushed open the door to make sure she hadn't just left.

She hadn't.

She was curled up on the bed, still dressed, deep asleep.

Tomorrow. I would try again tomorrow and I wouldn't take no for an answer.

Chapter 26

Toni

I woke up an hour early, or rather my body woke me up an hour before my alarm clock was scheduled to go off as my stomach tried to kick its way out of my midsection. My body was coated in a thin sheen of sweat and every time I tried to sit up, my stomach lurched did a high-kick and then a back flip before it lurched again. Moisture coated the inside of my mouth and I tried to swallow to get rid of the taste of nausea. "Mistake," I shouted to myself and jumped from the bed, making a beeline to my bathroom.

A few minutes of heaving later and I didn't feel better exactly but I no longer felt like I was going to be sick. It was just a general feeling of pure crap so I washed my face, put my hair up in a bun and tried to get dressed for the day. Try being the operative word since my stomach did another twirl and dance before I found myself bent over the toilet once again. After the third visit to the toilet

I was really tempted to tell Brady that I couldn't work today but I knew more accusations would fly so I dressed in jeans and a t-shirt, grabbed a bottle of sparkling water and went in search of my charge.

"Good morning, Toni!" Layla bounced in her chair with a welcoming smile.

"Good morning. Did you sleep well?"

She nodded. "I had a dream about my mom and me and I wasn't sad about it."

"That's great, kiddo. I'm happy for you." Thankfully Brady was nowhere to be found so we ate a quick breakfast of toast with peanut butter and bananas before getting the day started. "I'm not feeling too hot today so we're going to stick close to home. Are you a good swimmer?"

She let loose an exaggerated nod. "I'm the *best* swimmer. I can go almost as fast as my dad."

"Wow, that is fast." I searched my brain for other things we could do to fill the time and I settled on another activity that would take time. "But first, let's pack a picnic lunch and one activity to do after lunch."

"Okay!" Layla's excitement was enough for me to push through making sandwiches with diagonal cuts, slicing fruit and cheese and all the other things to make a picnic seem fancy to a little girl. The nausea returned in fits and starts but my stomach managed to hang onto my breakfast until late afternoon.

The pool at Brady's place was incredible with sun loungers set up on one side and accent chairs on the other side, perfect for sunbathing and relaxing. The pool house was small but well-appointed with drawers full of brand new bathing suits for men and women, a small fridge stocked with expensive sun creams and lotions. Just behind the hot tub was an outdoor kitchen space with a grill, stove and glass door fridge. "Wow, this is great. What do you think Layla?"

Her eyes were wide with shock as she took in the area that we'd both never seen. "Is this ours? We can swim here?"

"It's not mine but it's yours and your uncle's. Ready for a dip in the water?"

"Is it going to be cold?"

I laughed, steadfastly ignoring another wave of nausea. "Probably but the longer you're in the water the more you adjust to the temperature. Unless you changed your mind?"

"No," she shouted and then flashed an apologetic expression. "Sorry. I mean no, I haven't. I just wanted to know."

"Come on. Let's do it together so it's less scary." We stripped out of our coverups and stood at the edge of the pool.

"One," Layla began.

'Two," I continued with a smile.

"Three," she said and jumped straight in the water like a cannonball and when she popped up to the surface she was laughing. "It's not cold at all!"

Layla was right but I still took my time, going into the pool in small baby steps until I was waist deep and then chest deep in the water. I kept an eye on Layla as I floated the length of the pool while Layla swam and kicked and had a good time. The sun combined with the warm water was like the perfect band-aid. The sickness remained but it wasn't as bad as it had been all morning.

"Watch me, Toni!" Layla stood at the edge of the pool, toes curled over the edge and a determined look in her face as she watched the water.

"I'm watching," I told her with a smile. I kept an eye on her but the sickness returned with vengeance, making my belly do somersaults as black spots popped up all around my vision. I heard the splash of Layla hitting the water but it was muffled along with her laughter. Everything was muffled and the world started to tilt. "Oh no," I whispered just before everything went black.

I didn't know if seconds or minutes had passed when my eyes opened under water, but I swam up to the surface and gasped for air. *It was just a dizzy spell*, I told myself.

"Toni!" Layla shouted my name and her tone was so full of fear I started swimming before I knew where she was. "Are you okay?" The breathless question was like a kick in the heart.

"I'm fine," I told her in a soft voice, trying to reassure her with a hand to her back. "I'm a little sick today and I just got a little dizzy. It happens sometimes but I promise you that I'm fine." I pulled Layla against my chest and hugged her tight. "Don't you worry about me, little girl. I'm the adult which means it's my job to worry."

She was so quiet that I knew she wouldn't soon forget

what she'd seen. How could she when she'd already lost so much? I needed her to think about something else, anything else and I knew just the topic. "You're really okay?"

I nodded. "Yeah, I'm good. So good I want you to tell me about what kind of guitar you're planning to get?"

It was the perfect distraction because she spent the next twenty minutes talking about different styles and colors of guitars, the sounds they produce and even what the strings were made from. I smiled and listened but I made sure my feet stayed on the pool floor where they belonged. The afternoon stretched ahead long and lazy. We swam and I read while Layla drew and the next thing I knew, the sun sank below the horizon and it was time to go inside.

I felt exhausted, like I ran a marathon this morning and worked a full shift at a busy restaurant during the afternoon, or maybe played in a professional football game. My legs dragged across the grass and into the kitchen before making my way upstairs.

"Thank, Toni. Today was super fun," she said after we finished a quick bath to wash away the day. "Dad used to take me swimming."

I flashed a sad smile for the little girl who would only have memories of her parents. "I hope today made you remember him with a smile."

"It did," she admitted.

"Good, and I'm glad you had fun today Layla. Sometimes we have to stop and smell the roses."

Her nose wrinkled. "Why?"

I shrugged. "It's a way of saying to live in the moment and enjoy the little moments, like swimming with a friend or drawing under a bright and sunny day."

"Oh. Okay. I'll do that." She flashed another smile and fidgeted as if she didn't know what else to say.

I put a hand on her shoulder and guided the energetic little girl back down the stairs and to the kitchen. "How about we split a banana?"

"Okay!" She bounced up and down on her toes and turned those beautiful silver-blue eyes my way. "Will you stay for dinner tonight, Toni?"

Dammit, I should have known she would ask mostly because she asked nearly every damn day with hope shining in her eyes. "Sorry, kiddo. Not tonight. I need to get the progress reports done for this week. Maybe another night?"

"You always say that," she pouted.

She was right and I felt bad that my absence at the dinner table was felt so keenly. It was my own damn mistake for ever eating a meal with the family. It wasn't against the rules but I didn't do it generally. "I know and I'm sorry, but you have your uncle."

"Since those progress reports are for me, I won't mind if they're a little late."

I clenched my jaws so tight I think one of my teeth split in half. The last thing I wanted was to have dinner with Brady and pretend that things were all right between us when they weren't. He knew it too.

He doesn't care.

I shrugged and feigned rubbing my forehead. "Thank you for the offer but I'm not really hungry. Had a big lunch." I was off my game because at my words, a look of concern crossed Layla's face.

"Are you okay, Toni? Are you dizzy again?"

I froze at the question but I recovered quickly. "I'm not dizzy but I am still feeling sick so I'm going to lay down and cross my fingers that I'll feel better tomorrow. Okay?"

"You sure?"

"Positive," I said and tried for a smile that would make me sound believable to Layla. I knelt down and wrapped my arms around the little girl, giving her a tight, reassuring squeeze. "I'll see you bright and early tomorrow. Okay?"

She nodded but sadness lingered in her gaze. "Good night, Toni."

I ignored the heavy weight of Brady's gaze on me as I left the kitchen. He didn't get to be concerned about me, not anymore. Not that he ever truly cared anyway. I made my way up to my bedroom, crawled on top of the bed and I promptly fell asleep.

Sleep came easily which was a relief, it was just too bad that my dreams were full of visions of Brady, smiling at me. Laughing with me. Kissing me. Touching me all over.

It was the most peaceful yet torturous sleep of my life.

Chapter 27

Brady

Toni was sick? She'd gotten dizzy today? Why was this first I heard of any of this? If she was too sick to do her job then I should've been the first to know. She hadn't said a word, not that it surprised me at all since she hadn't said much to me for too many days to count, unless you counted greetings and farewells. And I didn't count that, especially since they were mostly for the benefit of Layla so she didn't have a clue that anything in her life had changed.

What was wrong with her and why hadn't she told me? As her employer, if nothing else, had a right to know. As Layla and I sat down for dinner an insidious thought worked its way into my brain. What if Toni hadn't said anything because she was setting the stage for another payday? A much bigger one?

Stop it, I told myself. Thoughts like that were how I ended up in this uncomfortable situation in the first place.

The truth was that I had no real, concrete reason not to trust Toni. She'd proven herself to be incredibly trustworthy and the problem was now that she could no longer trust me. I hadn't given her a reason to want to open up to me, in fact I'd given her plenty of reasons not to trust me with her body or her heart.

I wasn't able to get much out of Layla about Toni being sick other than a brief dizzy spell. It was clear that my niece was worried but she trusted Toni when she told her it was just everyday sickness.

I should just trust her too.

I tried, but I failed. All throughout dinner, my mind was stuck on what was wrong with Toni. What if it was something significant? What if she needed some kind of long-term treatment? Who would she go to for help? I was so focused on my curvy nanny that I absently agreed to Layla's request for two big cookies for dessert.

Still, after dinner I couldn't work because I was too damn worried about Toni. At bedtime, all I wanted was to have her in bed beside me, her curvy body curled around mine so that the scent of her skin lulled me into a deep and peaceful slumber.

When it became clear that sleep wouldn't come easily, I kicked off the bedding and got to my feet and went in search of a cold glass of water. I needed to do something about the Toni distraction. I needed to find a way to get her to forgive me or I needed to forget about her. I already knew forgetting her wasn't an option.

But luck was shining on me because I found Toni in

the kitchen, lit by the refrigerator in a pair of shorts that showed off her silky thighs and a tank top that showed off nearly all of her midriff. *This is my moment,* I said and crept closer until I could smell her fresh from the shower scent. "We need to talk."

Her shoulders stiffened and that was the only clue she'd heard me or that I'd startled her. She turned slowly, closing the fridge door, before her gaze settled on my face. Her green eyes studied my face carefully, folding her arms as if preparing for a fight. "Are you unhappy with my work?"

My brows dipped forward at her question. "What? No." I shook my head because I was anything but unhappy with her work. "You've brought Layla out of her shell and you've managed to bring us closer together. I'm grateful to you for that."

"Okay." That one word was clipped but it held a wealth of emotion and none of them were positive.

"About the things I said, Toni. I didn't mean it and I owe you-,"

She stopped my apology and shook her head. "You don't owe me anything Brady. I work here and you pay me for that service. It's the only thing you pay me for," she said, a hint of fire in her green eyes when she said that last part. "Besides all that, I think you meant exactly what you said so there's no reason for you to apologize. I know where we stand." She looked away as if she was hurt and I'd never felt more like a dirtbag.

"I didn't mean it," I insisted wholeheartedly but she

refused to hear me, keeping her gaze averted. "You have to understand that women haven't historically been interested in me as a person, Toni. Before I was rich I could hardly get a first date never mind a second one, so imagine my surprise when suddenly I'm one of the most eligible bachelors in the state."

"Poor Brady has beautiful women throwing themselves at him," she said and rolled her eyes.

"That's what I thought at first. But then there were hints dropped that we should go to *this* restaurant or make a stop at *that* jewelry store. We should go away to Paris for the weekend. And slowly it all started to make sense. They were willing to put up with me to access my money."

Toni folded her arms and stared at me, her gaze narrowed to slits. "And I asked you for all of that too, right?"

"No," I sighed. "But those experiences over the years made me cynical. Made it hard for me to trust people and it turns out that's a hard habit to break." I flashed an embarrassed smile because it was embarrassing to admit that to this woman who was always so confident in who she was.

"I get it," she finally said, her voice full of resignation.

"You do?"

Toni nodded. "Trust isn't easy for any of us who have been hurt which is pretty much most of us."

"I'm glad you understand." At her words, relief crawled over me and alleviated the weight pressing down on my chest and shoulders.

"And when you meet the right woman, you'll want to break that habit for her." Sadness colored every syllable. It darkened her eyes and flattened those full lips out to a tight, straight line.

The finality of her words rammed into my gut with the force of a fighter jet and the breath left me on a grunt. She really didn't get it, did she? I shook my head to clear it because this had to be some kind of alternative universe. "Toni." My tone was pleading but I reached out to her, she took a step back. "What if I *have* met the right woman?"

Her lips tugged into a smile that lacked any hint of humor or joy. "You haven't, Brady. If you had any interest beyond sex you would want me to know about your life's work. Your passion. Your business. That's what normal people talk about when they care about someone. But you don't and I'm a big girl, I can handle the truth. I don't need to be told twice. Or three or four times, either." She took two big steps to the right, just far enough out of my reach that I couldn't touch her again, and then Toni walked away from me.

Too bad for Toni I had a few inches on her and in two steps I reached out and tugged her wrist. "Toni, stop," I growled and pulled her back until our bodies were pressed together. The pressure in my chest loosened at the familiar position, chest to chest and hip to hip, when nothing else in the world mattered but me and her.

Her eyes widened and a gasp escaped between her pouty lips. I took advantage of the moment and fitted my mouth against hers, so hungry for a taste of her that I couldn't breathe, couldn't think straight. The moment our lips touched it was like I was home again. Everything in the world made sense and the ache in my chest disappeared.

She tasted like chocolate and strawberry lip balm and the moment her lips parted, I slipped inside her mouth, devouring every corner of her mouth. I laid claim to it because she was mine. She didn't know it yet and yeah she kind of hated me right now, but the way she kissed me back told me it wasn't too late.

Not yet.

Her arms snaked around my shoulders and she tattooed her body against mine, flicking her tongue against mine, nibbling my bottom lip while her fingertips played along my hairline, teasing the sensitive flesh and sending a shiver down my spine.

I deepened the kiss and she didn't protest, didn't pull away. Toni pulled me closer and opened her mouth to me, moaning as pleasure filled her body. My fingertips moved back and forth against her silky midriff and every shiver that stole through her, made my cock harden with need, with unsatisfied desire. I wanted this woman more than I wanted my next breath. I needed her.

Which meant I needed to make her see. I needed to make it right.

I pulled back slowly, pressing my forehead to hers. "I'm sorry I hurt you, Toni. It will never happen again."

"I know," she sighed and pressed one final butterfly kiss to my lips before she stepped back and sighed. Her gaze studied my face as if she was trying to memorize the details and then, without another word, she turned and walked away.

This time I didn't follow her, didn't call her back. I watched the slow and steady swing of her hips as she disappeared from view. She walked away as if nothing had happened, as if that kiss hadn't affected her the way it had me when I knew that it had. I felt the intensity and the desire in her kiss. "Dammit," I growled into the empty kitchen because what else could I do?

I didn't know yet but I spent most of the night wide awake plotting and planning what I needed to do to make Toni see that she was it for me.

She was the right woman.

Chapter 28

Toni

I sat inside the exam room a nervous wreck, fidgeting with the hem of my black jeans as I waited for someone—hell, anyone really—to come in and tell me what I suspected to be true but hoped it was a gigantic mistake. I managed to snag the last appointment of the day on a Thursday and now all I could do was wait. And wait.

And wait.

"Ms. Stafford, how are you feeling?" The young doctor stepped inside the room with a bright smile and shiny black hair that made me feel dull and lifeless in my all black ensemble.

"Nauseous and exhausted, Doc. You have good news for me?" I held my breath as the doctor inhaled deeply and let it out slowly. Definitely not a sign of good news.

"I can't judge the quality of the news for you, but we've done all the analysis and it looks as if you're pregnant, Ms. Stafford."

Pregnant. The word landed like an anvil in the room and it settled in my belly just as heavy. Pregnant. Of all the things in the world I imagined to be wrong with me—cancer, autoimmune sickness, exhaustion—pregnancy was near the bottom of the list. An oversight on my part, clearly. "Pregnant." I said it like it was a foreign word that I couldn't quite define.

"Yes. Close to three months based on hormone levels and your last period. Is this not good news?"

I sighed. "It's a surprise is what it is, Doc. That's all." I shook my head as the reality of my situation settled around my shoulders. Having a baby with a man who thought I was nothing more than gold digger. "What do I do next?"

The doctor rattled off words like *choices* and *prenatal vitamin regimen* and I barely heard any of it, just enough to grab the prescriptions and a card for my next appointment before I left the medical center in a daze. The fog didn't clear, not even when I found myself at Lucy and Dante's place, feeling out of sorts and uneasy.

"Toni? This is a nice surprise. Come on in." Lucy waved me in with a friendly smile that I wasn't sure I deserved.

But I was here so I blurted out the news. "I just found out I'm pregnant and I don't know what the hell to think or feel about it all."

Lucy smiled and tilted her head as she studied me closely. Too closely. "Is this good news or bad news?"

I glared at my closest friend. "It's not exactly good

news, I suppose but most of all, I'm shocked. But I have a plan, at least I think I do."

Lucy nodded and set an oversized mug of peppermint tea in front of me. "Okay, let's hear the plan."

I took a long sip of the delicious, piping hot tea until my nerves felt at least a little settled. "I'll put in my notice and move to California where I'll raise my baby. Alone." My heart clenched at the plan but it was the best plan for everyone.

Lucy's face scrunched into a frown. "You can't do that to Brady, Toni. Please tell me you know that."

I nodded because yeah I did know that. But I also knew something else. "I don't have a choice. If I tell him he'll accuse me of lying to get at his money and then he'll make my pregnancy miserable until he has the results which will show the truth. I don't deserve that." I wasn't sure if I'd ever have another child and it wasn't fair for him to ruin my experience because he doesn't trust women.

"Toni," she shot back in that motherly tone that was supposed to make me see the error of my ways.

I shrugged off my doubts. "Maybe in a few years I'll send him a postcard to let him know the truth and then he can decide what, if anything, he wants to do." It hurt my soul to think about leaving Layla and not spending every single day with her, but she wasn't my kid. I didn't have a right to her memories so I reminded myself that it was better that it happened now rather than later when I loved her even more.

"This is a bad idea, Toni. A very bad idea."

"I agree." Dante entered the kitchen with a sober expression on his face, not at all apologetic about eavesdropping. "I didn't react well and it took me some time to get on board with reality, but I did it."

"That's because you were in love with Lucy. This isn't the same at all." Brady and I were a fling. No, we were less than a fling with a few casual encounters. "You guys are no damn help at all."

Lucy laughed. "You mean we're not telling you what you want to hear."

I nodded. "That's what I said."

Dante and Lucy shared a knowing look before they burst out laughing.

"Look, Toni. Just don't do anything rash. Don't make any big decisions while you're feeling emotional and vulnerable. You're hurt and you're prone to kneejerk reactions."

I frowned. "Says who?"

"Says me," she shot back quickly. "Just give yourself a few days to re-examine the situation before you make a decision."

"There will never be a good time to hear that I'm trying to trap him for lifetime child support, or that I did this on purpose to get my grubby paws on his cash." I shook my head and my eyes slammed shut as the damn memory hit me again. "He accused me of whoring myself out, of sucking him off for a simple piece of jewelry or designer shoes," I growled, the hurt still at the surface, visceral and painful. He'd been deliberately cruel and I refused to repeat that.

"Dante accused me of trying to get with Alex because I thought he had a bigger bank account. It was equal parts insecurity and jealousy." She flashed a smile at her husband, who had the good grace to blush with embarrassment.

"Yeah well, I'm not as forgiving as you. And California is off the table because you know about it and I'm sure if he turned those pitiful silver-blue eyes your way, you'd cave and give up the details. I need a new plan anyway."

"I wouldn't," Lucy insisted. "Bros before hoes, except for Dante," she said and smiled lovingly at her husband. "He's my number one hoe so I'd tell him. But no one else."

Dante grunted a reluctant acceptance of Lucy's words which made us both laugh uncontrollably.

"Yeah well, I'll make a new plan and I'll call you when I'm there to let you know I'm safe. Just so you're not tempted to play matchmaker."

"I don't need to play matchmaker. If there was nothing between you then you'd stay."

"There's a baby," I growled. "That's enough of a reason to get the hell out of dodge before he accuses me of sleeping around or something worse." I shook my head, sighing with frustration. "Thanks for listening, both of you. But I haven't made any decisions." It was a lie, but a necessary one. I didn't want Lucy to feel like she was in the middle so I flashed my patented haughty smile as I pushed away from her kitchen table. "I'll figure it out."

Lucy wouldn't let me leave without a long hug that nearly brought tears to my eyes and I pretended to be unaffected as I hugged her back, waiting until I was in my car and driving back to Brady's mansion before I let the tears fall.

Chapter 29

Brady

"We're on track to launch in sixty days which means we need to kick marketing and promotions into high gear." The game was officially finished and in the testing phase to make sure there were no bugs or plot holes in the game.

"We have a schedule laid out already, which you should have in your inbox." Sierra spoke with confidence as she outlined the plan that had been approved for months. "Everything is on track. Don't worry, boss."

I let out a huff of laughter that I didn't feel. "I always worry," I told her. "But I trust you to do the right thing." Strange that I trusted Sierra implicitly when I hadn't been able to show Toni the same.

"You heard it here first, folks," Sierra joked. "I'll keep you updated, I promise."

I nodded at the computer monitor where the team leads all stared back at me. "I know." The phone screen on my desk lit up and then vibrated across the hard cherry wood. "I need to take this," I told them and ended the video call all at once. "This is Brady."

"Mr. Winsome, this is Serenity Woods, from-,"

"I know who you are, Miss Woods. How can I help you?"

She sighed and the hair on my arms and the back of my neck stood on edge. "I'm sorry to have to deliver this news but Toni has given her notice to quit her current position. It doesn't have often but it does happen and I promise you I will have a replacement immediately."

"No," I barked angrily and instinctively. "That is unacceptable."

"I agree but she's quitting the agency and she plans to move out of state. There's nothing we can do to change that fact, I'm afraid."

She was leaving. Instead of facing me head on, she wanted to get as far away from me as possible. "This is entirely unacceptable, Miss Woods." But it was more than that. "We have a twelve month commitment and it is still in effect. If Ms. Stafford leaves, I'll sue you both."

Serenity huffed out a shocked breath. "I'm not worried about me," she growled. "I've dealt with men like you most of my life. But I will speak to Toni and get back with you." She ended the call without another word and I smiled to myself, knowing Toni would hate me for it but I knew she would come around.

She had to.

I paced the length of my office, wondering what I

could do to get Toni to change her mind. She'd ignored me for weeks, which was as clear a sign as any that she wanted nothing to do with me, but I couldn't shake the feeling that this was an emotional reaction, that she wouldn't leave if she didn't feel something for me too.

When the phone rang and vibrated on my desk, it startled me out of my thoughts. "Yeah," I answered right away because I knew it would be Serenity.

She sighed on the other end of the line and worry buried in my gut. "I've spoken to Toni and she's willing to pay out the contract. She even offered to pay my legal expenses if it comes to that."

"What?" Now I was really worried. Toni had mentioned that she came from money but I had no idea it was that kind of money. "Can she do that?"

"She wouldn't have offered if she couldn't," Serenity said in a clipped tone.

"Why?" The question revealed more about me that I wanted Serenity to know.

"I don't know," Serenity said, her voice filled with sympathy. "But I'm sure we can both guess."

Shit, she was right. Toni was leaving because of me. Because I'd said awful things to her, because I refused to open up and share my life with her. It was all my fault that I was losing her. "Thank you," I growled and ended the call to Serenity. My heart pumped fast and hard as I flung open my office door and rushed through the mansion and up the stairs to Toni's suite.

Empty.

Of course it was empty. It was Friday she would be on her way to her apartment. *I could go to her.* I could but I didn't want to do that and more importantly I didn't want Layla to see us fighting so I decided to wait.

Monday morning was a long way off, but what I had to say could wait until then.

I knew she wouldn't return on Sunday evening as she had been before everything went to hell between us, but when Monday morning rolled around I was waiting for her in the living room. "Toni, a word please?"

She froze, her expression unreadable as she nodded and stepped inside the living room. Wordlessly she took a spot in front of the fireplace, folded her arms and waited for me to say what I had to say.

"I'm not letting you out of your contract," I began. "We still have six and a half months left on our agreement and you will see it to the end, otherwise I'll be forced to ruin you and Serenity."

Heat flared in her gaze and anger made her nostrils flare but still she said nothing for a long time. "That's really what you want?"

"It is," I lied easily. What I wanted was for her to *want to* stay here with me and Layla, to make a life with us. But she was trying to cut and run before I could make things right.

"Fine," she shrugged and walked away without any argument.

My brows knitted into a frown. That didn't make sense. Toni was a woman who argued simply for the sake of arguing yet she didn't put up even a hint of a fight.

I'm immediately suspicious but I shook it off because my cynicism and suspicion is how I got into this situation in the first place.

She wasn't leaving and I considered that a victory. A small victory, but one that gave me time to make it right between us.

Chapter 30

Toni

One month later

I hated that I was still in Houston. Still working for Brady. Still keeping a distance the size of the Grand Canyon between us. I had to do it because if he got too close he might suspect the truth. This way I could feign exhaustion and head to my room for the night, where I scarfed down sandwiches and salads for dinner rather than risk a midnight run-in with my boss and billionaire baby daddy.

At least I had Layla and watching her grow into herself was a total pleasure. She was so smart and creative, so sweet and trusting with her heart. Her love. She was a talented little girl and every time I thought about her major milestones—first book published, first art show, high school graduation—my heart pinched. But this wasn't my life. I was contractually obligated to be here for another few months, so I would be.

For Serenity's sake.

I refused to let Brady do anything to damage her business, especially when she'd been nothing but good to me all these years. She didn't deserve that so I decided to stay but the moment my obligation was complete, I would be gone. No matter what.

"Earth to Toni," Layla said as she stood in front of me giggling like crazy.

I blinked and looked around the carnival grounds with a smile. Layla and I were celebrating her enrollment into school by enjoying a day at the carnival. We'd already stuffed ourselves full of funnel cakes, corn dogs, street food and cotton candy, and now we played so many carnival games I knew we'd both have calloused hands in the morning. "That was a close one," I told her with a smile as she kicked my butt at the water gun horse races.

"I won!" Layla jumped up and down as if it was her first win and I couldn't help but smile, couldn't help the warmth that blossomed in my chest.

"You did. That means you get to pick the prize."

She tapped her chin and stared at the oversized stuffed animals on display. Her gaze lasered in on an oversized giraffe and after a few trade-ins of other toys, she was engulfed by the giant giraffe. "You like it?"

"It's great," I told her honestly. "Exactly what I would've picked." Except maybe not since I was the adult in this equation which meant I was responsible for carting Mr. Giraffe around the carnival grounds until we were ready to go.

We ate chili cheese fries with extra crispy bacon on top, which was incredibly delicious, and a horrible, bad, no good decision on my part because minutes later, heartburn made me feel like I was going to die. "Oh, shit." I put a fist to my chest as if that alone would stop the impending death feeling.

"Toni?"

"I'm fine," I assured the little girl. "It's just indigestion. Probably from the spicy chili." I smiled to make sure Layla wasn't worried about me because it wasn't her job to worry, but a second later I knew it was inevitable. My vision started to blur and not even a glass of fresh milk from a dairy stand helped.

"Toni," Layla shouted as my legs crumbled underneath me.

She was at my side, screaming and crying while I could do nothing but lay there and hope like hell that me and my baby survived whatever fresh hell this was. "Okay," I moaned weakly and patted her hair, hoping she understood that I would be fine.

At least I hoped I would.

When I wake up later, I knew I was in the hospital before I opened my eyes. The telltale sound of medical equipment, the low buzz of fluorescent lights and the steady hum of soft conversation surrounded me. *How in the hell did I end up here? Where is Layla?* That question made me bolt upright, where a wave of nausea sent me falling back against the bed. "Layla?"

"I'm here, Toni." Layla draped her body across my lap and hugged me tight. "I thought you were dead."

My heart squeezed at her words. "I'm sorry for scaring you but look at me, not dead am I?"

"No," she groaned as tears streamed down her pale cheeks. "I'm glad."

"Me too and I'm sorry that I scared you, kiddo." I hugged her closer and dropped a kiss on top of her head. "Sorry our carnival day got ruined."

Layla's laugh was watery but she shook it off. "It's okay. We can do it again when you get better."

"Definitely," I agreed as the door opened and a nurse in colorful scrubs walked in and sighed. "What's up," I asked with a hesitant smile.

"You're fine," she assured me before she launched into a whole spiel about needing new vitamins and more hydration. "The doctor has prescribed you a different combination so we'll see if that works."

"Thank you. Everything is, um, all right?" I slid a gaze to Layla to silently warn the nurse not to speak too bluntly.

"Yep. Everything looks good. Perfect, in fact."

"Excellent." I sighed and nodded towards Layla. "Is there anyone who can take her to get a snack after all the excitement?"

The nice nurse nodded and corralled Layla out of the room, giving me a few blessed moments to myself to think. To worry. To figure out what the hell I would say to Brady when he showed up, which happened far sooner than I wanted it to.

The door flew open and Brady strolled in looking handsome and worried and angry, a nurse right on his heels.

"What in the hell is going on?" His eyes were wide and his nostrils flared like an angry bull as he looked at me and then scanned the room. "Layla?" His gaze bounced around the room again, wide and worried. "Where is she?"

"Grabbing something to eat with one of the nurses," I sighed, more annoyed than I should be by his perfectly normal fear response. "She's fine. Safe and healthy, just a little scared from seeing me pass out."

His gaze finally settled on me as if he just now realized that I was lying in a hospital bed, hooked up to half a dozen monitors. "What's wrong?"

"Nothing that you need to be worried about."

"Bullshit," he spat angrily. "As your employer I have a right to know."

"No, you don't. I can perform my duties effectively and if you doubt that, well you can just fire me."

His nostrils flared faster and harder. His gaze narrowed. "You're in the hospital."

I shrugged. "Medical emergencies happen."

"Why are you being like this, Toni?"

I shrugged and looked away. "I don't know what you mean. My health concerns aren't anything I'd normally share with my employer. It's not necessary and since I'm contractually obligated to stay here, it doesn't matter. Does it?"

He growled, chest heaving with pure, unadulterated frustration. And then without a word, he stormed out of the hospital room.

I couldn't help it, I smiled.

Payback was a bitch but sometimes she was a funny bitch.

Chapter 31

Brady

"None of your concern, she says as if *that's* an acceptable answer." I grumbled to myself as I paced the hallway outside Toni's room. Her *hospital* room because Toni was in the hospital. And she wouldn't tell me why. "Dammit." Up and down the hall, I paced and scrubbed a hand over my face, grumbling to myself like a crazy person.

"Can I help you with something, sir?" A nurse laid a hand on my shoulder, probably to stop my incessant pacing, her brows tugged in concern. "Sir?"

"What? No, I don't need anything except answers which *she* won't give me," I growled and glowered at the door. "I'm fine. Really. Just worried."

She flashed a tight smile as if she understood, which she probably did because people inside this building were always worried about something. "There's a waiting room down the hall."

Of course. She wanted to get the crazy man out of the hallway. I was probably scaring off the patients. "Right. Sorry. I'm just...never mind."

Another nurse approached in a hurry with Layla at her side. "You must be the dad," she said with a smile as she shoved a bunch of papers at my chest.

"I am, yes." I frowned and looked from the nurse to Layla. "What is all this?"

"Discharge papers and new prescriptions for your wife."

My wife? "I think there's been a mistake." I looked down at the papers, barely hearing the nurse as she droned on and on, absorbing the words. Pre-natal vitamins. Pregnancy weight. Due date. Words I hadn't expected to see. My eyes grew wider with every word and then came the anger.

Toni is pregnant. No, not just pregnant. She was a few months along. Toni was pregnant and she hadn't said anything about it. *Maybe the baby isn't mine.* That thought stung more than it should have. I should be happy, but I'm not.

"Sir, is everything all right?" Now I had two nurses and one worried little girl staring at me like I'd lost my mind.

"Yeah everything is fine. Just fine," I growled and held up the papers clutched in my hand. "Excuse me." There was a pregnant nanny I need to have a talk with. "Is there something you want to tell me?"

"No," she answered quickly and looked away. "I'm

tired so feel free to take Layla home."

"I have your discharge papers and your prescriptions right here, Toni. Prenatal vitamins."

Her green eyes stared back at me with a blank expression and I thought she was just going to ignore me until she spoke. "It's none of your business."

"What did you say?" I shook my head and let out a bitter laugh. "I guess that answers my next question. The baby isn't mine."

She flinched. It was so small I wasn't sure I'd seen it at all because she recovered so quickly. "If you have to question it, you should get why this is none of your business."

"Uncle Brady?" Layla's voice was quiet and scared.

"It's all right, Layla." I turned back to Toni, anger still pulsing through me. "Were you ever going to tell me?"

She laughed and shook her head. "Why would I ever share such a personal detail with you when you won't share any details of your life with me?"

"This is not the same and you know it." How could possibly think this was the same?

"Fine, Brady, you want to know the truth? Here it is. I got pregnant on purpose. Or did I? Maybe I'm not pregnant at all and this is an elaborate ruse to get my hand on a few of your dollars. Maybe a car or apartment?" She shrugged. "Who knows?"

Her words hit me. Hard. Every syllable was like a punch to the jaw. The gut. The dick. "Toni." I sighed and rolled my eyes. "I never said that."

"Yeah," she laughed bitterly. "You did. Maybe not in

so many words but I'm a smart girl, I managed to read between the lines."

"We need to talk about this."

"No we don't." She folded her arms, big red lashes blinked quickly like she was trying to hold back tears, which made me feel like I was about an inch tall. "I didn't tell you because there is nothing to tell, Brady. I'm fine and I am not your problem."

"It's not a problem. You are not a problem."

"I know that, but I don't think you truly believe that. In fact, you should just take Layla home. And please, leave my papers here." She looked away again like that was it, her word was final.

I looked back at Layla who had tears streaming down her face and I realized, in that moment, that I had to shove my feelings to the side and put Layla first. "Come on, Layla. Let's get you home." I reached a hand out to my niece and something settled in my chest when she took it.

"I'll see you later, Toni. Right?"

She swiped at her tears and nodded. "Oh yeah, kiddo. I'll see you soon, I'm sure."

"This conversation isn't over."

"What conversation," she spat at me. "You said what you needed to say and there's nothing else to talk about. I'll come soon to clear out the space I'm taking up in your home and I'll send your lawyer a check for the broken contract."

"That's not necessary."

"It is," she whispered. "That's what you care about

most so I'll make sure you get it." Without another word she turned her back to me and tugged up the hospital sheet.

Conversation over.

For now. I vowed to give Toni a day or two to think about us and what we could be. During that time, I would do the thing that brought us to this moment in the first place.

Open up.

Chapter 32

Toni

The moment I'm released from the hospital, I hitched a cab to the now, almost-empty fairgrounds to retrieve my car. The rain made the grounds muddy but it took me about fifteen minutes to make my way through the expansive parking lot to my car. It was dusty but there was no damage and I slipped behind the wheel, letting out a long, slow breath before I jammed the key in the ignition and turned.

The next scheduled stop on my list was Brady's mansion. In the three days I'd been in the hospital getting my vitamins readjusted I had sent a check to his lawyer, put my condo on the market and started looking for a small, single family home that would be perfect for me and the baby. The only thing left to do was move out of the nanny suite and get on with my life.

It was easier than it sounded.

I took my time on the long drive up to the mansion and

when the door came into view, I sat for a long time and just watched the door, wondering what, if anything, was going on the other side. *This is it. I have to do this. It's time.*

I stepped from my car and took in the details of the mansion one last time before making my way to the front door, step by hesitant step. I sent a word of hope up to the universe that Brady wasn't home before I shoved my key into the door and twisted the knob.

The house was quiet, which was unusual but today it was a relief. I didn't have the energy—mental or emotional—to deal with Brady again. He knew the truth about the pregnancy but how he felt about it was a mystery to me. It didn't matter. He knew and he didn't seem happy about it, which made leaving this placement a good thing.

A damn good thing.

Part of me was tempted to stop in the kitchen first, to see Brady and Layla enjoying breakfast one last time but the new and improved me was determined to avoid temptation at all costs. Instead I went straight up the stairs but before I made it to my suite, I was stopped by a tall, hot, broody nerd with a gentle smile on his face. "Toni."

His anger was gone, which was a relief but it was also disappointing. I didn't expect him to fight for me but I maybe, sort of hoped that he would fight for our baby. "I'm not here to cause any trouble or fight with you Brady. I just came to get my things."

"Can we talk first? Please." Brady pressed his palms together, begging for a moment of my time.

Every nerve in my body urged me to say no, to tell him

that we had nothing else to talk about. But the pleading look in his eyes stopped me. I weighed my options. Did I really want to hear whatever he had to say or would it simply prolong the inevitable end? The inevitable goodbye. "Sure. Fine. What would you like to talk about, Brady?

He nodded, a sad look in his eyes. "I'm sorry, Toni. I owe you an apology, several actually. I haven't done much right when it comes to you and for that I am truly sorry. I let the fear of my feelings for you get in the way, thinking that if I ignored them, they would go away. I thought I could put you in the same box as every other woman and when I couldn't, I acted out."

I didn't know how to respond to that so I kept my gaze focused on his gorgeous face, unwavering yet uncertain about what came next.

"I thought you would just accept it, but you didn't. You kept pushing to get to know me and as much as it thrilled me, it also made me incredibly suspicious."

"That's pretty fucked up." I laughed nervously and Brady laughed in response.

"Yeah, it is." He scrubbed a hand over his face, his smile sheepish and brilliant. "It was unsettling, your desire to get to know me. If I had told you about me, then you'd know more and have more to use against me. If I didn't share, I risked losing you. There was no way to win."

I nodded at his words even as my blood boiled. "I didn't know this was a game. I just wanted to get to know you."

"I know and as much as I appreciated that and wanted to share parts of my life with you, I wasn't expecting you, Toni. It made me skeptical. I didn't know that I should expect a woman like you, sassy and fiery and vibrant, curious to know about me as a man, not just a multi-millionaire. A woman who liked me for me? It was a goddamn fantasy which made it even harder to believe."

"I never asked you for anything. Not once." Nothing other than details of his life and that, apparently, was too much to ask.

"Yeah and it was too unbelievable that a woman like you was genuinely interested."

"You keep saying that as if it's an excuse and it's not. You were deliberately cruel to me for no damn reason."

"No good reason," he added with a flash of a smile. "I didn't know a better way to process my feelings, which is no excuse, simply an explanation."

He made it difficult to stay mad at him, which was saying something because I could stay mad at people I didn't even know but it grew harder and harder to hang on to my anger. "You keep saying that you have these *feelings*, that you need to process your *feelings* but even now you're skirting around what those feelings actually are."

He stared at me like everything was so obvious, so crystal clear that I should already know the answer. I had my suspicions, despite his behavior, but I needed to hear the words. If there would ever be a chance at something more between us—and I was doubtful—he needed to say that words.

Out loud.

I waited and stared.

He stared back, stricken with fear.

I sighed and shook my head.

Brady continued staring. Staring yet not saying a word.

"Yeah, that's what I thought." I couldn't deny the disappointment that stole through me or the sadness that crushed down on my chest and made it difficult to breathe. "Goodbye, Brady."

Fear flashed in his silver-blue eyes and then shock that I was actually leaving and finally, heartbreakingly, resignation.

He accepted it.

Easily. Too easily, in my opinion.

Luckily I hadn't brought much to the mansion so packing everything up took less than an hour. It would have been done sooner if not for the tears that blurred my vision. Two sweeps of the room and I was confident that no trace of me was left behind.

There was just one thing left to do.

"Hey Layla, you have a minute?"

"Toni!" She jumped up from her little desk and ran over to me, wrapping her slender arms around my waist. "You're back!" She pulled back and smiled up at me, so happy and excited, her eyes so full of love.

I was sure the next few minutes would kill me. "I am back. For now."

I saw the moment my words registered. Layla's shoulders fell and her smile dimmed. "You're not staying."

"I'm not" I confirmed. "But that doesn't mean that I don't love you or that we can't still be friends."

She put more distance between us and folded her arms angrily. "I'll never see you again."

"That's not true," I insisted and pulled her close for a tight, near suffocating hug. "You can see me whenever you want, if your uncle says it's all right. I consider you a friend. In time you'll have more friends your own age and you'll forget all about me but I will never forget you Layla. Not ever."

Tears streamed down her cheeks and she shook her head. "Why? Why can't you stay?" Her words grew louder and more emotional. "Did Uncle Brady do something to hurt your feelings? I'll make him apologize and then you can stay. Right? Right, Toni?"

I sighed, swiping at my own tears because I felt out of my depth with her sadness. "I can't stay, Layla. But this isn't goodbye for me and you, okay? It's see you soon. All right?" Her tears gutted me and I held her tighter and kissed her cheek. "I'm sorry I let you down Layla but I promise you that I'm not gone forever. I promise."

Her sobs shook us both and never in my life had I felt so low. I promised Layla I wouldn't be another person to leave her and here I was, leaving. And not even for a good reason, for something as silly and as cliché as ever. Falling for the boss. "I love you, Toni."

"Love you too, Layla."

The little girl rushed back to her bed and cried like her heart was broken. Unable to stand it any longer, I grabbed my things and hurried from the mansion, eager to put this part behind me.

Chapter 33

Brady

"Dammit, what in the hell can I do to fix this?" It was a testament to just how out of my depth I was that I was asking my creative time for love advice. I stared at the monitors, each contained an image of Sierra, Cal and Tori in their individual offices. They all stared back at me, half-terrified as if they were concerned I was on the verge of a nervous breakdown. "Well? Anyone have any ideas? Please."

Blank stares met my words and I started to squirm in my desk chair. Sierra spoke first. "At the risk of pissing off the boss, why didn't you just open up to her? I mean, we all met her and she seems awesome. Funny and spunky and not scared of your growly face."

"I don't know," I shouted. "Because I'm an idiot?"

"A scared idiot," Cal added, a defiant tone that wasn't at all helpful.

Sierra rolled her eyes and I made a note to give her a

raise. "Was Brady acting like a scared little girl? Yes. But," she grinned and my scowling face. "He does have a shot at redemption."

"I do?" I asked, incredulous.

"He does?" Tori and Cal asked simultaneously.

"He does," Sierra confirmed. "But only if you're willing to open up to her."

"I can do that," I said eagerly. "I will do that."

"Good," she nodded and flashed a confident smile. "But this isn't going to be easy. Toni won't be satisfied with dumb trivia like your favorite color, most memorable concert or the dessert that always make you think of dear old mom. Nope." She let the word pop with emphasis just to make her point. "You're going to have to offer up the goods, the ugly and the dirty details of your life, and hope she hears it and forgives you."

"What if there isn't anything ugly or dirty?"

Three sets of eyes stared back, each one silently proclaiming me a liar. "There is," they all said at once.

I sighed, half annoyed because they were right and half annoyed because they were smug about being right. "So, what? I'm supposed to just cut myself open and bleed for her and then what, hope for the best?"

Sierra flashed a wide smile. "Congratulations, Boss Man, you finally understand." Her proud grin would've grated on my nerves if I hadn't specifically asked for her help.

"As much as I'm loathe to admit it," Cal began, "Sierra is right. If you want your woman back you'll need to be honest with her. Share the details of your life that you don't ever share."

I let out a heavy sigh as their collective advice weighed on me. "Tell her everything and hope for the best?" It wasn't an ideal option, in fact the idea of opening up like that made me physically ill, but I couldn't deny that their advice was sound. "You're sure this will work?"

Cal barked out a laugh first. "No, we're not sure. Not at all, man. But it's your best shot. Anything else is guaranteed to fail."

"Seriously?"

Tori nodded first.

Sierra joined in, a sympathetic expression on her face.

Cal nodded, a solemn look on his face. "Seriously, Brady."

"Well, shit." If that was what I had to do, then I would do it. The past week without Toni was pure hell. It was a living and breathing circle of Dante's hell. The house was too quiet, too melancholy without her lively personality, her bright red hair and her sassy attitude. Each day that passed without Toni was torture. Layla was inconsolable without her favorite person. She refused to engage with me because clearly it was my fault she now had to live without Toni.

Everything in the world was worse without Toni. The sun didn't shine as bright. The sky was a dull imitation of her usual glory. Music didn't have the same pizazz it usually did. Nothing was as fun without Toni as it was with her and in general, life fucking sucked without her.

Which meant I needed to open up.

"What are you gonna do?" Sierra's question was hesitant but she wore the same wary expression as the others.

"I guess I don't have a choice, do I? Sharpen the razor blade because I'm going slice myself open and hope it's enough for her."

"Perfect," Sierra said, her words encouraging. "Be honest about who you are and speak from the heart. Toni seems like a woman who will respect that."

She would respect it, but would she forgive me and take me back?

Only one way to find out.

"Thanks, guys. I owe you for this."

"I accept payment in crypto," Tori said with a smile.

"Just get her back," Cal offered with a shrug. "When you're happy, the rest of us can be happy too." With those words, the conference call ended and I was left trying to come up with a plan to get my baby mama back.

Chapter 34

Toni

"Are you sure this is the right course of action?" Lucy's question was well-meaning and I knew she wanted me to get the same happy ending that she'd gotten with Rush, but she was just in her own little love bubble.

"No Luce, I'm not sure at all. But this is the path laid before me which means that it's what needs to be done. House hunting because the idea of a living space without a green space for my baby is just horrific."

"Horrific? Hyperbole, much?" Lucy laughed and when she rolled her eyes I regretted the video call.

"It's not hyperbole. I'm pregnant and what happens if the elevator breaks down? I'm not dealing with that shit. And I want my kid to have somewhere to run and play and get dirty. Is that so wrong?"

"No," Lucy sighed. "It's not wrong. But if I recall,

Brady's place has plenty of green space that would be perfect for a growing kid."

"It would be. In fact, it is perfect for the kid he already has and wants. Layla." He'd given no indication that he wanted anything to do with this baby. "I can't force him to want something else, Lucy. I won't."

She sighed, exasperated. "Men are stupid, Toni. How many times have you said that to me?"

"Enough times," I grunted.

"Exactly. Brady might not have said what he meant in the most eloquent way, but did you really give him a chance?"

"Yeah, I did. I gave him multiple chances to tell me what he felt, what was in his heart and he couldn't do it." That was just as bad as if he'd rejected me outright. "No matter how he feels, his fear is greater than his feelings."

"Ugh," she rolled her eyes and shook her head. "See? Stupid. They may be strong and brooding and sexy, but above all else they are incredibly stupid. Remember that."

Her words made me smile. "I will never forget again," I promised just as a knock sounded at the door.

"Oh! Did you order birria tacos? Please say yes and let me watch you eat them!"

I laughed. "I wish, but morning sickness is kicking my ass. It's probably a relator who somehow sensed I was putting my condo on the market and wants to *take a peek*."

"Good luck," she called out with air kisses before she ended the call.

The knock sounded again and I frowned at the door,

wondering who had the audacity to show up at my place without an invitation. Annoyed and heartbroken and angry, I marched to the door and pulled it open with a scowl "What the hell do you want?" My heart caught in my throat because it wasn't a pushy realtor and it wasn't Molly who was supposed to stop by today. "Brady."

He flashed a shy smile and nodded as he shoved his hands deep into the pockets of jeans that hugged his thighs and hung low on his hips. "Toni, hey."

I folded my arms and did my best to look uninterested and intimidating. "What are you doing here?"

"A few years ago I dated a woman, Nina Katarova. She was beautiful and just a little bit geeky, the perfect woman for me. Or so I thought." Brady sucked in a deep breath and scrubbed a hand over her face. "She liked a lot of the things I liked so I was eager to learn about some of the things she liked that were foreign to me. I tried Russian cuisine and even attended Fashion Week. I thought we were in love, moving towards the bigger picture, you know? Engagement and marriage and family." He laughed bitterly. "Until I heard her saying that she could put up with a lot for a seven figure bank account. It gutted me, at first. And then it made me angry."

My heart ached for Brady. He was a good man with a lot of positive traits that had nothing at all to do with his wealth. He was gorgeous and funny, slightly grumpy and so damn sexy even now my body responded to him. "She sounds like a total bitch."

His lips kicked into a lopsided smile. "She was," he

agreed. "But it took me a long time to realize that she was the problem and not me."

"Sounds like low self-esteem," I diagnosed and stepped back, motioning for him to come inside.

"That was part of it," he admitted easily. "Mostly it was that I was so blind, possibly willfully so that I ignored the signs. The suggestions of where to go for dinner or an impromptu vacation, what kinds of clothes I should wear and events we *needed* to attend. So I closed myself off. Shuttered my heart and stole my faith in women, and in myself."

My arms folded protectively over my chest and I stared back at him, ignoring the desire that welled up inside of me to forgive him and jump into his arms to make us both feel better. "I never asked you for anything," I said for what felt like the thousandth time.

"You didn't, but still I waited for the other shoe to drop. You were too beautiful and sassy, too lively and confident to actually want someone like me."

"But I did, Brady. I wanted you. I wanted to *know* you, but that's not what you wanted so tell me why you showed up here on my doorstep?" I needed to know and I was desperate for answers.

"You want to know why I'm here?"

I nodded.

"I thought it would be obvious but since it's not, let me be clear that I'm here for you Toni. I love you. I am madly in love with you and I fucked it up so bad that I came here to see if I could make it right."

My heart stopped and did a backflip inside my chest at his words. No, they weren't simple words, they were a declaration. "Pretty words."

"It's true," he said and took a few steps towards me. "I understand why it might be hard for you to believe, but it's true. I fell in love with you and I tried to keep us in a little bubble forever so that I could keep you." Ge barked out a bitter laugh and shook his head. "I loved you so much that I couldn't risk learning that you were like all the others because I knew I was too weak to walk away from you, so I kept us frozen in amber."

"You didn't' give me a chance," I argued.

"I know! It was stupid and I will forever be sorry for the hurt I caused you, but I was so damn scared of losing you that I lost you anyway." He took a few steps forward so he was just close enough to brush his fingertips along my bare shoulders and arms. "But I'm here now because I love you, Toni. I love you and I can't live without you but more than that, I don't want to live without you. Life is boring as fuck when you're not around."

His words were music to my ears but like Brady, I still had my doubts. "Is this about the baby? Because I won't keep you from the child."

"No, it's not about the baby. At least not how you think. Let's just say that the news of the baby was a wake up call for me to get my head out of my ass before I lost you forever."

"Talented baby," I joked and absently rubbed my still —mostly—flat belly.

"How could it not be with you and me contributing DNA?" He smiled and I couldn't help but smile in return because he was handsome and charming and he owned my heart. But I wasn't an easy sell.

"And the next time doubts creep in? Am I going to find a stack of one hundred dollar bills on the nightstand?"

"No, never," he promised and gathered my hands in his. "Doubts won't creep in, not ever again. I love you Toni and if you want a trip to Paris or Milan, Tokyo or anywhere else on this plant or another, it's yours. What I have is yours, including or most especially, my heart."

I folded my arms and ignored the rapid beating of my heart. "And if I say that I don't want any of that? That your money and status don't impress me?"

He wrapped an arm around my waist and pulled me close. "Then I hope like hell that you find me impressive enough on my own to deal with those things."

His words yanked a laugh from me and my forehead fell against his shoulder. "Oh, Brady. I love you too."

"You do?"

I nodded. "I'm impressed by what you've built and how you're still so passionate about it, but that's not what I love about you." I sucked in a deep breath and let it out slowly. "I love that despite being out of your comfort zone, you took Layla in and tried to make her feel at home. I love that you're this beautiful, powerful man and you have no idea just how appealing that is. You're this big insecure nerd with the world at your feet and that is so incredibly sexy."

He laughed. "You're a weirdo, you know that?"

"It's been mentioned a time or two," I shot back with a smile as my heart hammered against my chest. "But I'm a weirdo who loves you."

"And I'm the luckiest damn man on the planet because I love you too and I want to build a life with you Toni. Me and you and Layla and our new baby too. More if that's what you want. Tel me you want that too."

My lips parted into a grin I was powerless to stop. "I want that too and I want it all with you, Brady Winsome."

"Brady Lionel Jessop Winsome," he shot back with a sheepish smile.

My brows shot up in surprise. "That's a mouthful, but I like it."

"Yeah?"

I nodded. "Almost as much as I like you."

He frowned. "You said you love me."

"I do, but I also happen to like you. It's important for a healthy, long-lasting relationship."

His breath caught and his gaze heated. "I like you too, Toni. A whole hell of a lot."

"Good. Kiss me."

Brady leaned forward and pressed his lips to mine and then I was lost completely to the soul deep kiss that stole my breath and held my attention. Brady was a powerful man with the world at his feet, but he was also just a man with his own fears and insecurities. It made him more human, more beautiful, and that vulnerability took up a bigger spot in my heart than I expected.

Who knew the man of my dreams would be wrapped up in a sexy, nerdy package with as many issues as me? As much as he didn't expect me, I hadn't expected Brady either but I am damn glad our paths crossed.

He was my future. My next step.

My chance to make the family I always wanted.

He pulled back with a smile and scooped me in his arms. "Bedroom?"

"Right here is good," I panted. "Right here. Right now."

In just a few quick moves, Brady's pants were around his ankles, my panties were shoved to the side and he entered in one long, powerful stroke. "Ah, so fucking perfect." His hips began to move in long, deliberate strokes that made my vision blur and yanked me closer and closer to the edge. "I missed you and I missed this."

"Me. Too." I grabbed his ass and pulled him deeper and harder, so hungry for him I could taste it.

A rapid knock sounded on the door and we both groaned. "Who is it?"

"Realtor," I panted. "I'm putting the condo on the market to get a bigger place for me and the baby."

"Fuck that," he growled, pulling out slowly before he surged forward in another long, powerful stroke. "You belong with me. Rent this place out," he demanded.

"You sure?"

His hips never stopped moving. "Positive."

I smiled. "Okay."

"Okay?"

I nodded again. "Okay."

"Go away," he shouted. "Not for sale." With a predatory smile, he gripped my thighs and took us both to the top of the mountain where we jumped.

Together.

Epilogue

Toni ~ 5 months later

"I can't believe I found the perfect window where none of you are pregnant, or at least showing." I smiled the three women gathered to help me get married to the man of my dreams today. "That has to be a good sign, right?"

Lucy tossed her head back and laughed. "You're ridiculous, you know that?" Her hand went to her belly, telling me that I was in fact, right.

"How far along?"

"Three months," she admitted as a blush crept up her cheeks.

"Four and a half months," Sasha added with a laugh.

My eyes widened in shock and Molly laughed. "If it makes you feel better, I'm not pregnant at all. I'm single and horny and unemployed so there's that."

I bit back a smile. "I'm sure none of those will last much longer," I told her with confidence. "And the unfairness of it all is that you look smoking hot on *my* wedding day."

Her cheeks turned an adorable shade of pink. "Right. We need to get you in this chair where you will stay for the next hour. Got it?"

I smiled at this bossy side of my friend. "Yes ma'am. I like you all feisty like this." I sat for the next seventy minutes while the hair and makeup team made me look fabulous for my wedding day. My red hair was pulled up into an intricate updo with plenty of sexy tendrils to drive Brady wild. "Okay, we're done right?" The team nodded and I stepped from the chair with a grunt. Being seven months pregnant wasn't the ideal time to get married but Brady refused to wait. He was determined to get married before the baby arrived so here we were, having a simple yet elegant backyard wedding.

The girls helped me into my dress which was white and lace and it made my boobs look amazing. "You look gorgeous," Molly said near tears.

"I do look pretty damn great, don't I?"

"I'd marry you," Sasha said with a laugh.

"I'd kiss you with tongue inside a church," Lucy added and we all laughed until the team chided us as the touched up our makeup.

The door flew open and Layla stood there with a wide-eyed smile. "Toni you look like a tough princess!"

"Well that makes me feel even hotter. Let's get me married!" I grabbed Layla's hand and tugged her into the middle of our hug huddle. "In an hour, I'm going to be Mrs. Toni Winsome. Can you believe it?"

"That's how weddings work," Molly added with a frown that drew another round of laughter from all of us.

We all lined up and made our way to the doors that led to the backyard. My heart raced and the baby kicked in my belly, but I wasn't afraid. Nope, I was ready to merge my life with Brady's.

The vows flew by and then my lips were fused to Brady's while our small group of loved ones cheered and whistled their congratulations. "That was one hell of a kiss, husband."

Brady flashed a wide smile. "It was just the first kiss of the rest of our lives." He kissed me again, this time tipping my pregnant body over his arm and deepening the kiss until I felt the answering tug in my belly and lower. "Love you, wife."

"I love you too, my sexy, nerdy husband."

His nostrils flared and he pulled me upright with a proud smile, lifting our hands in the air while the cheers grew louder. "We have exactly twenty minutes before we're obligated to do wedding photos. It was a gift from your mother," he whispered in my ear.

"Twenty minutes?" I looked around and saw Layla had taken up residence on my dad's lap because apparently all they needed to get off my back was a loving grandchild to spoil.

"Yeah. Do you need to do...anything?"

"Yeah," I nodded slowly. "Just one thing. My husband."

Brady grabbed my hand and dragged me up the makeshift aisle and into the house. We made it to the bridal suite on the first floor before we made love for the first time—of many—as man and wife.

"Have I told you how gorgeous you look today?" Brady kissed my shoulder as he fastened the buttons on my dress.

"Only a half dozen times. You're slipping, Mr. Winsome."

His laugh sounded rich and deep in my ear, the sound vibrated against my back. "You take my breath away, Mrs. Winsome."

I turned in his arms and kissed him one last time just as the knock sounded on the door. "And you make me wish this baby was already here so I could show you how hot you look in a tux."

He laughed. "I have one more secret for you, Toni."

"Yeah? I'm listening." Over the past few months, Brady had dropped all kinds of information about himself all over the place.

"Our wedding song is by one of my favorite artists. Norah Jones."

"Unexpected, but I dig it."

"That's not all."

"We're married now, Brady. You don't have to keep doing this."

"I know but I love it." His smile was wide and beautiful and it took my breath away. "I'm going perform the song for you."

My eyes widened. "You're going to sing?"

"I am. But I'm also going to play the piano because that's something else about me you don't know."

My heart was so full I could hardly breathe at this admission. "I can't wait. But I have something to tell you too. My dad is a twin."

He frowned. "Okay. Thanks for sharing?"

My head fell back and laughter exploded out of me. "Remember that appointment you missed last week?"

He nodded. "It couldn't be helped."

"I know and I understand. But we're having twins. Twin boys."

He dropped to his knees and wrapped his arms around me, nuzzling my waist. "Seriously?"

I nodded. "Seriously. Feel free to share it during your performance later."

He pressed a soft kiss to my belly before standing. "You are the best gift the world has given me, Toni. I'm so happy you're my wife, my life, my everything."

Tears pooled in my eyes but I refused to get another damn touchup before photos. "I love you, too. And if we make it through these photos without going crazy, I see a quickie in your future."

His nostrils flared and he took my hand, dragging me to the photographer where we finished wedding photos in record time.

The journey was off to a good start and I was confident it would only get better.

* * *

THE END

Check out the other books in the **Curvy Nannies for Single Dads** Series by scanning the QR code:

Preview: Midlife Do Over

A Step by Step Guide on How to Derail your Career in Fine Dining at the Age of 40:

Hit an egotistical, megalomaniac star Chef over the head with a leg of lamb.

That's it. The End.

It certainly ended my career in Chicago and landed me back in my small town to lick my wounds.

And right back into the arms of my next door neighbor.

Ryan Gregory, reclusive country rock sensation, and my high school sweetheart.

It might be chemistry, but it certainly wasn't love.

So sure, now I'm going to have his adorable baby in a few months.

But I wouldn't let it be love, not ever again with Ryan.

So sure my best friend is conspiring against me, planning our long overdue happily ever after.

There is no way I'm serving up my heart on a platter to Ryan. Again.

So sure he looks even more delicious now than I remember.

I know the truth, Ryan has never seen me as anything more than a groupie.

So why can't I get the man to stay out of my backyard, my bed or my fantasies?

Prologue

Pippa ~ 2 Months Ago

"Thank you for visiting Graze today. I hope you had a wonderful meal." I flashed my most dazzling smile at the clearly less than impressed couple, waiting patiently for them to speak.

The couple stared at each other with a worried expression before the woman turned to me. "The asparagus was delicious, buttery and perfectly firm. The mashed potatoes were a little bland, and the steak was just okay. But we didn't want to complain."

That would be a first for the crowd Graze drew on a daily basis. "Feedback is always welcome," I assured them with a friendly grin.

"That's not a goddamn julienne! Open your eyes or get the hell out of my kitchen."

I kept my smile tight while the couple listened in clear horror as Chef Rodrick unleashed yet another tirade on a kitchen employee. "He has high standards." It was the best I could do to attempt a defense of the chef's unacceptable behavior, but the couple's eyes went wide, and they hurried out of the restaurant. Probably never to return.

Oh well.

Chef Rodrick had been on a tirade all shift, verbally abusing the kitchen staff, barking angrily at the waitstaff as if they were the reason his food was coming out of the kitchen in substandard quality. He had the temperamental and egotistical parts of being a professional chef down to a science. It was just too bad that his food fell flat if everything didn't go perfectly, which it never ever did in a professional kitchen. He'd been hired at Graze almost a year ago, and frankly, I didn't know how he still had a job except for he could be charming when reporters were around and he was easy on the eyes.

Too bad he's not easy on the ears.

I was the front of house manager for Graze, had been for the past three years, but it was only the past twelve months that had been a hellish nightmare. But Rodrick was a star, allegedly anyway, which meant the rest of us had to grin and pretend as if the kitchen wasn't run by a complete psychopath.

"Excuse me, miss?"

I let out a sigh at the one title no woman over the age of forty wanted to hear. Miss. It just felt like a commentary on my sadly single-in-the-city status. Chicago was a city of almost nine million people, and I couldn't find one solid, single man to date. But that wasn't the customer's fault, so I turned with a mostly professional grin and headed to table three, located near the front windows with a view of Michigan Avenue. "What can I do for you folks today?" I glanced around the table and did a double take at the man with the silver goatee who I was pretty sure was the famed restaurant critic Paul Renault. He could make or break a restaurant with a few taps of his keyboard.

"How was the leg of lamb?"

The woman with a short black bob and a pinched expression answered for the table. "Not good, sweetie."

I gave my obligatory frown and nodded. "I'm so sorry to hear that, what can I do to make your dining experience better?"

"We'd like a new lamb, cooked properly this time. Please."

"Absolutely, I'll let the chef know. Would you like a complimentary glass of champagne while you wait?"

"Absolutely," the man I was pretty sure was Paul Renault replied with a relieved groan.

With a polite nod, I turned away from the table and headed towards the kitchen. Before I pushed through the swinging doors, I sucked in a deep breath and let it out slowly, reaching for a calm I didn't feel knowing that an interaction with Rodrick was imminent.

You got this. Even if you don't, it's your job.

My little pep talk did nothing to stop my racing heart, so I did what I always did when times got tough, I stood a little taller, pushed my shoulders back before I balanced the platter of lamb in my hands, and forged ahead. The kitchen was a beautiful sort of chaos, the way all pro kitchens were. It was that song and dance that had drew me to the world of fine dining, this craziness that produced the most delicious, beautiful, artistic edible creations known to man. I loved it.

Usually.

"Get the hell out of my kitchen! Now!" Chef Rodrick's roared words didn't intimidate me in the least, but the rest of the kitchen fell mute.

This will be a lot easier since he shouted at me first, I told myself as I fixed a bland expression on my face, the platter resting on my palms. Being nice to Rodrick never paid off anyway.

"Gladly. As soon as I let you know that this leg of lamb is dry."

If possible, the kitchen fell even quieter as the chef whirled around, his whites still pristine after hours of working, and sucked in a breath.

"Excuse me?" The disbelief that he could have possibly cooked a dish imperfectly was laughable given the complaints I fielded this shift.

Instead of using the diplomacy I always tried for when dealing with sensitive and temperamental chefs, I smiled. "As dry as the Sahara."

Rodrick laughed. "I don't have time for your silly games, Pippa. Go back to the front of the house and worry about doing *your* job."

Dear Lord help me find my calm. I let out an exhausted sigh and stared at him in those deep green eyes. "Table three wants another lamb because this one is dry. So *dry* they couldn't eat but a few bites each." I put extra emphasis on the word dry because that vein in the middle of his forehead was already pulsing and that amused me. "Just fix it because-,"

He cut me off before I could tell him who the lamb was meant for. "My lamb is not fucking dry. I don't cook anything dry, so go back out there and tell your precious customers that's how the lamb is cooked." Rodrick shook his head and swiped a dismissive hand in my direction. "Just stay in your own damn lane, Pippa."

I nodded, not at all unaccustomed to chef's belittling my work, as if dealing with the customers wasn't as important as the food they ate. "Whatever. You do what you want Rodrick, but the customers who paid for this leg of lamb says it's too dry to eat." I held up the platter and the sous chef moved to relieve me of the heavy piece of meat, until Rodrick held up a hand to stop him.

"Tell them to try it again."

I shook my head. "Maybe you should try it, because they did, and it was, quote, *not good*."

"That's not possible."

"That's funny, because to those three customers it's more than possible, it's reality." Reality that they overpaid for what amounted to lamb jerky, from their perspective.

Another bark of laughter sounded, this time derisive, and I knew another tirade was coming. "This coming from some backwoods hillbilly who's spent a little time in fine dining establishments? Excuse me if I don't bow down to your culinary expertise."

"No, excuse me for thinking a chef might pull out a meat thermometer when all the customers say their steaks are too dry, or too rare. It's not my culinary expertise they come for, it's yours, and lately that is in serious question." I was done arguing with this idiot who clearly didn't have the sense the good lord gave him.

"Yeah?" Rodrick stood at six-foot-four and decided to use his considerable height advantage against me, looming above me as if I was supposed to be scared.

My heart raced, but I ignored it, too fired up to worry that today might be the day he lost it completely. "Yeah. Everything tonight has been overcooked as hell, but you're incapable of taking any kind of criticism, so no one tells you, and the waitstaff gets stiffed on good tips. Because of you. Not some backwoods hillbilly, but the allegedly classically trained man-child dressed in his chef's costume."

"Take it back," he growled.

"Get out of my face, Rodrick."

He smiled because he knew he had me at a disadvantage with the cumbersome platter of meat in my hands. "If I don't?"

I set the platter down on the expediting strip and turned to face him. "I'm not one of your kitchen slaves, I bite back." I shook my head and took a step away, not in defeat, but retreat.

Rodrick's hand reached out and grabbed my arm, causing a collective gasp among the kitchen staff. "Get your hands off me, Rodrick." My heart thudded against my chest as my flight or fight instinct kicked in. "Let. Me. Go."

"Don't walk away from me."

"Get your damn hands off me. I won't tell you again." He laughed and gave my arm a tight squeeze, a look of utter glee in his green eyes. He was getting off on hurting me and the yelp I let out when he squeezed even tighter, pushed me into action. "Ow!"

"Right," he snorted. "Or what?"

What happened next, in hindsight, was ill-advised at best, but I was a southern girl at heart, and no one got to lay hands on me without paying the consequences. I grabbed the leg of lamb and swung it at Rodrick, hitting him right in his stupid, smug face. He hit the ground with a grunt. "Or you'll regret it."

He smiled up at me. "I regret nothing. You're done here. Pack up your shit and get out."

I smiled down at him and shook my head. "Maybe so, but that lamb you refused to make again? Was ordered by Paul Renault. Good luck getting your next job." Without another word, I turned on my bright red heels and returned to the dining room.

At the end of my shift, I finished up my responsibilities and called my best friend, Valona, who still lived in our hometown of Carson Creek, Tennessee. "Hey Val, it's me.

There was a moment of silence before she spoke. "Pippa. What's wrong?"

"Other than the fact that my chef is the world's biggest

jackass? Not much." I gave her an abbreviated version of the shift from hell and sighed with exhaustion. "He actually said, *you're done here.*"

"Pippa, what if he's serious?" Valona was a natural worrier, about anything and everyone in her orbit. As a single mother to my adorable goddaughters, she didn't stop worrying even when she was asleep.

"Oh he was, but Rodrick doesn't have the power to fire me. That doesn't mean I won't get fired, just that I'm not yet."

"What are you going to do if you get fired?"

I let out a frustrated sigh. "What do you want me to do, Val? He grabbed my arm and squeezed it. Hard. Twice."

"You did the right thing, but what will you do if you lose this job?"

"I'll figure it out." The same way I figured out my life when I was eighteen and the future I thought I would have, vanished right before my eyes. "Hang on, another call's coming in. Wish me luck."

"Good luck, honey. Love you."

"Thanks." A deep breath and I switched to what I was sure was The Call. "Hello?"

"Pippa." I recognized Josh Wiseman's nasally voice immediately. "You hit Rodrick with a leg of lamb."

"He grabbed my arm and hurt me, Josh. He had no right to put his hands on me."

"I agree, Pippa, but I can't keep you on. You understand?"

Preview: Midlife Do Over

I nodded, nostrils flaring as my anger built. "Yeah, you think he's the next big celebrity chef. But let me tell you, Paul Renault might disagree with you."

"What does that mean?"

"You'll find out when the rest of Chicago does."

Josh sighed. "Let's not make this ugly."

"Oh, I won't make it ugly, honey. Trust me." I let out a sigh and flashed a smile at myself in the rearview mirror. "But my lawyer might."

"I wouldn't do that if I were you."

"Yeah? Well I wouldn't keep an abusive prick on staff who is a lawsuit waiting to happen. Talk soon, Josh."

"Valona, you there?"

"I'm here. Are you fired?"

"Yep. And I'm suing. Wish me luck." Lord knows I'm gonna need it.

Chapter 1

Ryan

O ne Month Ago
I looked around my hometown after being away on tour for the past ten months, and smiled. Carson Creek was as small town as small towns came, complete with a Main Street lined with big red oaks, wooden sidewalks and American flags flowing in the wind on every business. Colorful awnings, sale signs, and people actually chatting with their neighbors.

Carson Creek was home. Had been since the day I was born and no matter how far I traveled, what I had experienced on the road, it would always be home. Home. The word took on new meaning when you spent most of the year touring the country, and the world. Things that used to bother me, the gossip, the way everyone was all up in everyone else's business, the lack of secrets and late night delivery, suddenly seemed charming. Even endearing.

That's why I did what I did. I had taken a step to ensure that my stay in Carson Creek would be permanent. I bought a restaurant. What in the hell did I know about restaurants? Nothing at all. I was a simple man who preferred burgers and fries, steak and potatoes to things like sushi and fine wine. But I was a quick study, had learned to play the guitar on my own as well as the piano, and became a pretty good songwriter without any professional training.

Most of all, I had time. The tour would be over soon, which meant I could focus on writing the next album and learning the ins and outs of running a successful restaurant.

I maneuvered the car to the dead end street that led to the Old Country House property where my restaurant was located. The long driveway was reminiscent of those big old properties where generations of families lived at the same time, except this was an oversized events' venue, which provided the restaurant with guaranteed business. From a business perspective it was a smart move to make, and my name recognition would—hopefully—help increase bookings.

It was just how Carson Creek worked, everyone chipped in to help out everyone else.

Damn, it's good to be home.

The long entrance split into three roads, the one on the left led to Dark Horse, the restaurant was named after the first song I wrote that went double platinum. It was my biggest achievement at the time, considering Derek was the lead singer and Roman was the showman. It was still my pride and joy, played at bars all over the world, drunk patrons singing along with my lyrics about being underestimated by a love interest.

And now it was a living breathing thing. A place that was just mine, not The Gregory Brothers.

I stepped from my Jeep that was older than dirt, and smiled at the sight of Mayor Carson, arms folded but smiling broadly. "Ryan Gregory. Good to see you." He extended a hand to me and I accepted it with a grin of my own.

"Still weird that you're the mayor, but it's good to see you too, Chase." I still remembered him as my girlfriend's pipsqueak little brother with his nose stuck in a book.

"It's my third term, Ryan, about time you got used to it. Especially now that you're a business owner." He nodded over his shoulder to the brick building with Dark Horse scrawled across the front, complete with a Stetson wearing stallion as the logo, even though I was no damn cowboy.

"Third term, huh? Good for you."

Chase rolled his eyes. "You donated to my campaign, Ryan."

"Me? Can't be true." I shrugged it off because the kid was good at his job. I didn't spend much time in Carson Creek these days, but the gossip still managed to reach me.

"How's it feel to be back in town? You've been gone a while this time."

I nodded, acknowledging the truth of his words. "Been too long if you ask me, but this tour is major for us." After so long in the game, it was a gift to be so popular, to adjust to the digital age of music and streaming, after two decades in the business. "Feels strange, but good to be back, which pretty much sums up life in Carson Creek." It was always an odd mix of relief to be someplace familiar, and anxiety about being around people who knew everything about you.

Chase laughed and shook his head. "A sentiment I understand completely." He clapped me on the back and there it was, that sense of relief that came whenever Chase was kind to me. Civil. His sister hadn't forgiven me for leaving to pursue my dreams. Still.

"I'm excited to come back for an extended stay once the tour is over, though."

The sound of heels clacking behind me drew my attention to Margo Blanchard-Devereaux, the owner of The Old Country House, the business and the actual house. She wore a pale pink suit with matching heels, walking at a fast clip as if she was always in a hurry.

"Ryan. Mayor. Sorry I'm late, I had a panicking bride to deal with." Type A to the core, Margot smoothed over her pristine clothes and hair with a sigh. "Good to have you back, Ryan."

"Temporarily," I added with a smile for an old friend.

She flashed a proud smile, the one I'd gotten used to

over the years as the whole town took pride in the success of the wild Gregory brothers. "How's the tour going? I read somewhere that the last two weeks sold out in just minutes."

"Yeah, the crowds have been amazing." It's not that I was uncomfortable talking about my work, my songs and music, but touring was part of the job. Enjoyable for the fans who came to hear the live version, to sing along and have a good time. Ticket sales was for the studio to worry about.

The conversation fell flat, and Margot, never one to endure awkward silences, clapped her hands briskly. "I'm excited to see the inside of this place. Your assistant has been very tight-lipped," she added with a frown. "Very."

I laughed. "Devon is efficient and loyal." My assistant didn't do anything he didn't want to unless it was about protecting my image and privacy, and I'd given explicit instructions that I wanted to see the finished product first.

"Yes, well, he is that," she added haughtily and looked up at the restaurant sign with a frown. "I still wish you would have chosen a different name. One that's more customer friendly."

I sighed, wondering if the built-in business would be worth the hassle of Margot's constant needling. The woman had to have everything her way or she fell apart, but this was my baby. My business. "I can always find another location so you won't have to see such an eyesore, Margot."

She blinked in shock, eyes growing round at my harsh

words because everyone in town went out of their way to be polite, even when it wasn't warranted. Recovering quickly, Margot brushed off my words with a smile. "Just some friendly advice."

"From your long tenure in the restaurant business?"

Margot was saved from scrambling for an explanation when the doors of Dark Horse opened and Devon appeared, with a welcoming smile for everyone except Margot. "Looks like we have a crowd." His questioning gaze slid to mine, and I knew he was wondering if this group counted as me laying eyes on the restaurant first.

"It's fine," I assured him with a sigh. I wanted time to look at the place on my own, to give it a thorough examination so I could sit with it, figure out if it was what I wanted for my first foray into real world investments. "Input is always welcome. So is word of mouth promotions," I added with a grin.

Satisfied, Devon nodded and took a step back to wave us all inside. He hung back and fell into step beside me. "I've hired an amazing chef who is the perfect blend of modern fine dining and southern home cooking. She's from Knoxville, but trained in New York and Italy. She's also provided me with a mile-long list of kitchen staff." Devon nodded to the stack of papers on the bar. "I've got more applications than I can handle, which brings me to the most important hiring decision. Front of House manager."

I paused and quirked a smile at him. "More important than the chef?"

Devon shrugged. "Good food doesn't matter if the service is crappy or there aren't enough waitresses to meet demand."

"Good point." One I hadn't thought about. "What do you need from me?"

Devon froze and stared at me like I'd grown a third eye. "This person will have to be someone you trust, someone you can get along with, especially if you plan to stick around for the foreseeable future."

Oh. Right. "Make sure it's a local who knows how things work around here. Someone with restaurant experience and someone who won't just say yes to me even when I don't know what the hell I'm talking about."

"Seriously? You want me to hire the person for this position?"

"Why not? You hired the chef."

"That's because you wouldn't know good food if it jumped off the plate and bit you." His smile softened his harsh, but true, words. "You can sample her cooking if you're curious."

"I will, but later though. I trust you."

"This place is stunning," Margot practically shouted across the empty dining room.

At her words, I was finally able to give the place my full attention. Devon had done his damnedest to bring my vision to life, and he'd succeeded beyond my wildest dreams. The Dark Horse dining room was a strange mix of old school saloon and modern fine dining with dark wood tables and matching floors, the long bar was a shade darker than the other wood finishes, drawing the eye first. The chairs were heavy with burgundy leather upholstery and decorative wooden studs instead of metal or brass. Dim lighting gave the place a cool, exclusive feel and the fancy wiry chandeliers that hung above each table let you know this was a place where you could expect great food for your money.

"Well? Don't leave me hanging, boss."

I smiled at Devon. "I love it."

"You do?" He looked around and pointed at the mirrored bar stacked six shelves high, the leather stools bolted to the floor in front of the bar. The wildflowers inside small wooden vases in the center of each table. "You love it?"

"Yeah," I sighed. "I wouldn't have picked this stuff myself. Hell, I wouldn't have known to pick it, but it all works. You did a good job, Devon. A really good job."

His shoulders sank in relief. "I'm glad to hear that."

"I'm happier to be able to say it." There was so much that went into opening a restaurant and I didn't know half of what I needed to, not yet, but I would. As soon as the tour was over and I came home for good. "What are we looking at for opening day?"

"A month or two? First I have to hire a manager and together we'll have to hire front of house staff, settle the menu and specials. Shouldn't be too long after you get back."

I did a double take at his words. "Me? Why do I have to be around for that?"

Preview: Midlife Do Over

"Because, Dark Horse, you are the main attraction. People will show up just for a chance to lay eyes on the quietest Gregory brother, and hopefully they'll stay for a steak, a bottle of whiskey or a three course meal."

Ah, dammit. "Right." It was high time I got used to being part of the sideshow. I'd spent my entire career doing it in the background, happy to let Derek and Roman soak up the spotlight. But this business was mine, which meant the song and dance for customers was mine to perform.

It was a small price to pay for a much-needed distraction from the fact that I was getting too old to be on tour nonstop.

Chapter 2

Pippa

~ **T**oday

"It shouldn't have come down to this, Pippa." Josh sat across a small table and looked at me with disappointed eyes, a look that had, for years, compelled me to work harder and longer hours, to do my absolute best to impress him. Today that look only fired up the anger that had mostly subsided over the past two months. "If you had just let me fire you and left quietly, you'd still be able to work in this town."

I laughed. "Oh please, Josh. Don't act like I'm the only one that took a big hit with your attempts to blackball me. Sure some of the chefs who prefer to run their kitchens with a heavy dose of abuse don't want to deal with me, but how many restaurants want to hire your former golden boy?" I looked at my lawyer who sat beside me with a stoic expression and shook my head. "I mean, it's lunchtime in downtown, and there are what, maybe five tables occupied today? Seems to me you fired the wrong person."

"Graze will be just fine."

"Eventually. This town has a long memory, especially when powerful men gang up on a woman just protecting herself from physical abuse." This town, I learned the hard way, also had a low tolerance for tattletales, which apparently I was. Twelve interviews in two months had resulted in nine different versions of, "don't call us, we'll call you." Three at least had the guts to tell me they didn't want the publicity of hiring the infamous Leg of Lamb Lady.

It was all vague promises that meant nothing, which meant I was done in Chicago.

Josh smiled smugly. "I've had a few calls for references."

"Yeah and you told them nothing but lies. Thanks for that." I held my hand out in a *gimme* motion. "I'll have my checks now, though."

That wiped the stupid smug smile on his face. "Hope this money is worth the damage you caused."

"You made your choice first, Josh. Remember that. When this place starts to circle the drain, think about the fact that you were happy to keep a man with a history of physically abusing his employees, his coworkers and his girlfriends, over a loyal employee. I hope that thought keeps you warm at night."

Josh let out a long, exhausted sigh that told me I'd hit the mark. "Severance," he said and pushed the check across the table. "And settlement check."

"Thanks. And I won't hold it against you that you tried to make me homeless by withholding my severance pay for two months. But I will wish upon the first shootin' star I see that you get exactly what you have coming to ya. Later." I pushed away from the table and turned on my heels, stoic attorney at my side, and walked away with my head held high.

"You did great."

The attorney speaks! I looked up at him with a wide grin and held out my hand. "Thank you, Mr. Griffith. You made this entire process less scary than I imagined."

There was a flash of a smile on his lips before it disappeared. "You didn't need my help, but this case put me on the radar of the partners, so thank you."

"Good luck."

"Same to you." Inside the parking garage, we went our separate ways and I ignored the shakiness of my legs and let out a long sigh as I looked over the railing and out to the city, gray and drizzling. Even horrible weather couldn't stop Chicago from moving forward. It was one of the things I loved about this place. It's why I'd made it my second home. Fifteen years, three fine dining establishments and one chain restaurant job under my belt, but now I was leaving this place behind.

It didn't feel right to leave under these conditions, but thanks to Paul Renault, the whole city knew the truth, that I wasn't some emotionally abusive basket case. A hot head, he'd called me, which was just as bad for a front of house manager, so it was still the kiss of death. Temporarily, anyway. So, instead of working my way back up in this city, I decided to leave. To pack up my bags, my apartment, my whole life and head back home, to Carson Creek.

Tennessee here I come!

I hadn't been home in more than five years. It was too risky. My heart still too fragile. More than twenty years had passed since the love of my life had told me he was leaving town, without me, and still it was too raw. It didn't help that memories of him were all over the town. Wild child made good was a great redemption story in a town that craved a happy ending.

Now, avoidance was, well unavoidable. I could only hope that luck was on my side and he was on some stage on the other side of the world. Of course, he would be back—eventually—and I would deal with that, with him when the time came.

But on top of my priority list was finding a job. A place to live and a paycheck. At forty, I was right back where I started. No, I was worse off than when I was a brokenhearted eighteen year old, because at least then I was running towards a new future, a new life. A new, unknown adventure.

Now I just felt as if I was moving in reverse. Going back home with no job, no prospects for a job, divorced after a short-lived marriage, and my tail between my legs. It felt like failure.

A big fat freakin' failure.

Ten hours and only two bathroom breaks later, I rolled

past the Welcome to Carson Creek sign and felt the knot in my belly grow tighter with each passing block. Each southern red oak tugged my smile a little brighter, and my belly a bit more anxiety-filled. This was my home and I missed it terribly.

So much, that every sign of familiarity made my heart ache, clench with regret that I let one little heartache keep me away for so long. I missed years with my best friend because phone calls, emails and video calls just weren't enough. Not when my goddaughters were growing like weeds and growing into their personalities.

As I pulled up to Valona's three story Victorian, I smiled, suddenly very happy to be back home. To be with the people who knew me best in the world, my best friend and my brother, once again. They knew me, knew my heart, and had been with me during the best and worst moments of my life. Despite my absences, they didn't hold it against me, and most of all, both had welcomed me back with open arms.

And I would reward them by not being a burden or a distraction from their busy lives. I would spend a night or two with Valona and the girls, catching up and loving on my bestie and her sweet girls, and when I woke up tomorrow I would get started on the rest of my life. Starting with a home of my own and a job.

Not necessarily in that order, but a big fat failure couldn't be too picky.

Chapter 3

Ryan

"Holy shit man, that was the greatest show on Earth!" My youngest brother, Roman, clapped me on the back as we rushed off stage after a third encore, and made our way down the well-lit tunnel until we reached the main door of the backstage area. "That was the shit, and you know it! Don't even bother denying it." Roman entered the room, not at all nonplussed by all the women, the strangers lounging among our stuff as if they belonged.

It was still unnerving to me, but I was a little older than Roman's thirty-three years. He still found joy and escape in slipping it inside of a random chick anywhere there was a modicum of privacy. I didn't judge him for how he chose to unwind, it just didn't do it for me anymore.

Unfortunately.

While Roman got sucked into the clutches of two

wannabe groupies, I sat back, feeling good as I watched the partiers wearing wide smiles as if they had any claim on the kickass performance we put on tonight. For my part, I felt bittersweet, the same way I felt when we finished recording an album, performed the last day of a tour, ended a relationship. It was all just another ending to me, good while it lasted, but there was no desire to go back once it was over.

Except that once.

Derek and Roman soaked up the attention, as they always did. Whether it was women or genuine fans, they ate up every moment of it. Not as if it were their due, but as if it could all go away at any minute. Derek had a rapt audience as he recounted the way he felt when all fifty thousand concert goers sang along with him to *Always In My Heart*, while Roman whispered sweet nothings to a redhead and accepted small promising kisses from a blond.

I sat back the way I always did, and observed every little detail. Not in a creepy way, at least not to me, but I was a people watcher. It helped me write songs and stay grounded.

And now, I was ready to get the hell off the road. To sleep in my own bed with the brand new memory foam mattress, every night. It was a luxury I'd learned years ago to never take for granted, the pleasure of lying down on the same pillow in the same bed night after night. There was a certain sense of comfort in that kind of sameness, and no place offered that level of comfort, of sameness, as Carson Creek. It was home, it was where I could unwind, enjoy and just soak up the beauty of the place, let it soothe my restless heart. Let it inspire me.

That was my goal for my stay at home, to write songs for the new album, to relax, and learn all that I could about the ins and outs of running a restaurant. It wasn't exactly the rock star behavior people expected, but thankfully I was the boring brother. The quiet one. The old one. *Old, my ass. Forty wasn't old, not for me. I felt better today than when I was thirty, damn those bloggers.*

"Hey man, watching everyone like a creeper instead of enjoying the last night of the tour?" Roman's deep voice, filled with amusement, slowly pulled me from my thoughts, my plans for the future.

I shrugged off his gentle ribbing. "It's what I do."

"Luckily, you're almost as hot as me, or else it would be damn creepy." Roman laughed again and pulled a cold beer from a nearby cooler and shook his head as he twisted the top and took a long sip.

I let out a sharp bark of laughter at our familiar banter. "You wish you were as hot as me. Maybe after your balls drop, you'll come close." Roman flipped me off, as he always did, and then handed me a beer.

"What are your plans now that the tour is over?"

Good question. I hadn't told either of my brothers about my new investment. "Carson Creek. Maybe a few changes to my house, writing for the next album, and keeping a close eye on my new investment."

Roman's blue eyes widened. "A new investment and

you didn't consult me? Or Derek?" He let out a low whistle. "I think I'm offended."

"Don't be. It's a restaurant, not your thing."

"Not *my* thing? This coming from the guy who lives on peanut butter and jelly rather than trying carpaccio or kale." He shook his head, slapping his knee as he was overcome with laughter. "Not my jam, but if any one of us could make it work, it's you." I gave him a *don't bullshit a bullshitter* look and Roman chuckled. "I mean it. You're so serious and those lyrics that have sustained us all these years, they come from a deep thinker. Not shallow pricks like me and Derek."

He wasn't wrong, but I knew my baby brother better than I knew anyone else in the world. I'd taken care of him when our Mama died weeks after giving birth to him. Changed his dirty diapers, taught him how to walk and how to charm a woman. And yeah, he was definitely up to something.

"All right, drop the shit, Ro and tell me what you want."

A loud guffaw of a laugh erupted from his rangy frame, tugging a reluctant smile across my own face. "Me? Your baby brother, and I can't even compliment you at the end of the longest tour known to mankind without suspicion? Now I *know* I'm offended."

I rolled my eyes because Roman wasn't a cruel man, but he wasn't a serious man either. "What do you want, Ro?"

He sighed and stared at the packed backstage area,

his eyes landing on everyone but not really seeing anyone in particular. "I want to do a solo album." He let the words hang in the air for a long time, like he was waiting for me to explode or talk him out of it. I kept silent. "I don't want to leave the band, but I want to do more. Our next album isn't due for a year, what the hell am I supposed to do with all that free time aside from get myself into trouble?" He laughed. "You think I'm an asshole?"

"Nah." I shook my head and turned to look at my brother, really look at him. "I think you know that you don't do well with a lot of downtime and if you want a career away from us, you should go for it."

"Seriously?"

"Yeah, seriously. As you love to remind me, you're young with a lot of life ahead of you. You tell Derek your plans yet?"

His blue eyes, identical to mine and Derek's, and our older sister Lacey, widened almost comically. "You kidding? I want to enjoy this last night of the tour, possibly my life. I'm telling you because," he sighed again and turned to me.

"Don't keep me in suspense, Roman."

"It would mean a lot to me if you wrote some songs for me. For my voice." He flashed a smug smile at my surprised expression. "See? I was being totally genuine with my compliments."

I couldn't deny that Roman's words floored me. Not that I lacked confidence in my ability as a songwriter, just that, I guess I never let myself think too hard about what my brothers thought of my skills. "Me?"

"Hell yeah," he nodded and took another swig from his beer. "Who else?"

"Literally anyone else. Nashville is filled with songwriters looking for their big break."

"Yeah, but they don't have the depth that you do, and they don't know my voice better than the man who taught me to sing and play the drums." He looked at me, hope and expectation darkening his blue eyes. "What do you think?"

I didn't know what to think, but the truth was I could use all the distractions I could get over the next few months, and Roman was my baby brother, practically a son to me. "Ask me again in a week after I've had time to relax and unwind, you know, after the longest tour known to mankind."

His face pulled into a wide, satisfied grin. "Thanks, Ry."

"I didn't say yes."

"No, but you didn't say no, and we both know that means you're halfway to yes."

"We'll see." He was right, but he was too smug for his own good, and it was good for him to wait, to sweat it out before getting the answer he wanted to hear.

"All right, fine," he conceded. "I'll be knocking on your door in a week. One week, Ry."

"Not a moment sooner," I told him as he pushed off the seat beside me and sauntered back over the stacked redhead with the hungry green eyes and blonde with the pouty lips and barely there dress.

I stood soon after, grabbed a bottle whiskey from the table and left the backstage area and the concert venue, sparing one final, wistful glance at the perfect send-off. Without a word to my brothers, I made my way back to the hotel and slept peacefully, knowing it would be the last hotel bed I slept in for months.

Chapter 4

Pippa

"The first thing on my list is to find a job." It felt ridiculous, no, it felt pathetic to be starting over at forty years old, but this was my reality and I was determined to make the best of it. "A restaurant job would be ideal, but at this point I need to start earning some money."

Valona's big sage green eyes narrowed in confusion. "I thought you just got your severance pay and a big fat settlement."

"I have it and it's going in the bank today, well as soon as I have an actual address. But I can't live off that money forever, Val." As far as I could tell, there still weren't many restaurants in Carson Creek. It had given us the perfect excuse to make the hour long drive into Nashville every weekend as teens. "I was hoping to stay here, but if that's not possible, there's no point searching for a house."

Preview: Midlife Do Over

"There is an option, but I'm not sure if you're gonna like it." Valona's face was etched with worry.

"I'm listening. Tell me everything."

Valona nodded and got up from the kitchen table, her long legs taking a direct path to the coffee pot which she brought back to the table. "There's a property on Mulligrew Drive called The Old Country House."

"That overgrown eyesore on the dead end street?" That place had served as fodder for our childhood imaginations, and then a semi-secret place where we could drink and kiss boys when we shouldn't have been.

"That's the one. It's no longer overgrown or an eyesore. Margot bought it and turned it into a whole events complex."

"Like a wedding venue?" I shook my head. "I don't want to oversee caterers, Val. Is that even a job?"

She smiled and shook her head. "This is much bigger than that. Margot owns the land and the gorgeous plantation house the property is named for, so she gets a cut of everything. Carlotta Montgomery is the event planner. She specializes in weddings, but she does it all from debutante balls to bar mitzvah parties, bachelor parties and even divorce parties. I take photos for the events, usually on the property, but sometimes the couples want engagement photos and when I find studio space, I'll do them there when the situation calls for it." She smiled proudly, and it was downright contagious.

"That's great, Val! It's like guaranteed business for your new business."

"Thanks," she answered shyly, a small blush staining her cheeks. "Anyway, there's a restaurant on the property that's open to the public, but will also be used for events. The place is new and in search of a manager."

That was music to my ears and I felt excitement pulse through my veins. "Seriously?"

Valona nodded.

"Way to bury the lead, woman!" I reached for my phone at the end of the table. "What's the name of this place." Valona was silent and I looked up with a question in my eyes. "Well?"

She nibbled her bottom lip before pushing the words from her mouth. "It's called Dark Horse."

"Cool name. Is it some type of saloon? Never mind, found it." The photos of the place were spectacular, decorated in dark wood and burgundy leather. "It's fine dining?"

"It is, with a bit of a rustic flair."

My leg started to bounce excitedly. "Val, if I get this job then I can stay here in town, spend more time with you and the girls." What are the odds that a fine dining restaurant would open up in small town Tennessee just as I was looking for a job in fine dining? "It's kismet," I declared and stood up. "I have to go there. Right now. Is this a situation where you have to know the right people?"

"As far as I know you can show up with your resume. But Pippa, there's something you should know."

"I have to find something to wear. Something that

looks like I'm a pro, but that I can fit in with the people of Carson Creek."

Valona laughed. "You *are* the people of Carson Creek, Pippa Carson."

"You know what I mean. I haven't lived here in a long time and some might consider me too citified." I stopped in the doorway and waved Valona along. "Come help me pick out something to wear. Please?"

"Fine, but there's something you should know about Dark Horse."

I waved off her concern with a literal swipe of my hand. "Nothing can be as bad as dealing with Rodrick."

"I wouldn't be so sure about that," she mumbled, but I was already heading down the first floor hall to the guest room.

Inside my room, I pulled open the first suitcase I found, relived to see it was stacked with work clothes. "Black won't work, I think I need to wear something colorful. Something delightfully southern."

"Delightfully southern?"

"Yeah, you know, something colorful and feminine. But capable." I pulled out my favorite red slacks that hugged my backside like a lover. "How about this with my black silk top? It says capable and strong but feminine, right?"

"Yes. With those insane black stilettos you'll look gorgeous. As always."

I rolled my eyes at my best friend's compliment.

"Thanks, but I'm just interested in looking like a good front of house manager." I changed quickly and then dug through the lone box that wasn't sitting inside a storage locker, and found my power stilettos, capable of turning any woman into a superhero. "How do I look?"

"Like the world's best front of house manager?"

My shoulders relaxed at her perfectly placed words. "Thanks. Hair?"

"Keep it down," she said and closed the distance between us, scrunching my natural waves with her fingers. "Perfect."

"If I get this job, you, me and the girls are going out for dinner tonight. On me." I hugged Valona and held her in my arms for a longer than necessary. "Thank you for bringing this up."

"Don't be silly, I've just got you back in town and I'm not ready to lose you to the big city again."

"That's not going to happen. I'm sorry I stayed away for so long and missed so many years with the girls. It feels silly in hindsight, to let him keep me away for so long, but after things fell apart with Dexter, it just brought it all back to the surface."

"It's all right, Pip, I understand. Randy died in the middle of divorcing me, so trust me when I say that I get the baggage. If not for the girls having a solid community here, I would have gone away too."

I squeezed my best friend a little tighter. "I'm so happy I get to hug you anytime I want now." I pulled back with a smile, kissed Valona's cheek and rushed out the door with my black purse flung over my shoulder, car keys fisted in my hand. "Wish me luck."

"You won't need it," she called after me and I let those four words boost my confidence as I took the short drive to The Old Country House, which was even more gorgeous than the photos, and took the left lane that led to Dark Horse.

I sat in my car for exactly one minute, calming my breaths and giving myself a quick pep talk. "One jerk of a chef in Chicago doesn't define you. You know your stuff and you are an asset to any restaurant smart enough to give you a chance." I let my eyes connect in the mirror and smiled. "You got this."

I rushed inside, lest anyone else show up and try to take the job that was—clearly—meant to be mine.

Less than a minute after I entered, a long and lean man in a three piece navy blue suit with merlot window pane pinstripes strolled out to greet me with a pleasant smile. He looked as if he'd stepped right from the pages of a fashion magazine, which put him dressed even more fancy than me. "Welcome to Dark Horse. What can I do for you today?"

I put on my biggest welcoming smile and held out a hand. "I'm Pippa Carson and I am your new front of house manager."

"I'm Devon," he said with a hint of a smile and motioned me to a booth in the middle of the dining room after I handed him my resume.

I look around the place, excited about making my mark

on a brand new restaurant. "The décor is beautiful, a bit rustic, but no doubt this is a fine dining establishment. It has character and that can go along way for helping a new restaurant stand out in a crowd." I was rambling, I felt it down to my core, but I couldn't seem to stop myself. "This place will do good business even without the built-in help from the events taking place on the property."

"Tell me about Chicago." His words were short and to the point, delivered without emotion.

I nodded, feeling my nerves rise as I recounted the events that led to my demise in a clipped, emotionless tone. "The chef, Rodrick, grabbed me by the arm and then squeezed when I told him to let me go. He didn't, so I hit him with the leg of lamb he refused to redo for a paying customer." I shrugged as if getting fired didn't still burn. "The lamb was dry and he wouldn't hear of it, refused to even taste it and instead got physical with me. It wasn't my finest moment, but he's the only temperamental chef to ever get that reaction out of me."

The man, Devon, stared at me for a long time, probably trying to figure out if I was a diva or a crazy person. My hope started to fade the longer the silence persisted, but I kept my spine straight and my shoulders squared, projecting a confidence that dwindled with every passing second.

"Do you consider yourself difficult to work with?"

"No, and I don't think anyone I've worked with in the past, other than Rodrick, would disagree. I pay attention to culinary trends, both in food and décor. I'm great with customers, listening to their needs and cooling tempers without running to the chef constantly or giving away the whole menu for free. I expect a lot from my staff because that's what fine dining requires, but I'm easy to get along with as long as you do your job." I sighed and prepared myself for what he would say next. "I won't let myself be bullied or demeaned, no matter how talented the chef is."

Devon took in my words and nodded before a smile lit up his face turning him from average to good looking. "Excellent to hear. You'll love Chef Nina, she's as quirky as her food, and she's more of a hippie chick than a bully."

I nodded at his words before understanding dawned. "I will? Does that mean that I'm hired?"

"It does. On a ninety day probationary period, of course. Either of us can part ways with in that time for any reason at all. If you make to the ninety-first day, we'll start with a one year contract."

"Oh, wow. Thank you, Devon. I promise I will not let you down." My heart raced inside of my chest like I'd just finished a marathon. This was my second chance, one I desperately needed. "Thank you."

"No thanks necessary. I need a solid house manager, and aside from that one incident, your credentials are good. I'll double check them, obviously, but barring any deviant behavior, you have the job."

I accepted his outstretched hand and shook it with far more enthusiasm than I probably should have. "Do you have a set schedule, or are you a hands-off owner."

"Neither. I'm not the owner, I'm his assistant."

"Oh. You're so well-dressed, like every owner I've ever met." It was like they had to make sure we all knew they wouldn't lower themselves to do anything to help out in the front or back of the house.

"Thanks. I try." Devon sighed and handed me a stack of papers. "The owner will be home in a few days, but you should expect to take the reins around here as we get ready for the Grand Opening."

Take the reins? "Is he, um, does he..." I snapped my mouth shut before I insulted a man I'd never met.

"He is new to this business, this industry, but very eager and determined to make this place a success," Devon supplied helpfully. "When can you start?"

"As soon as you need me." I had a job. Not even twenty-four hours in town and I could tick one item off my to do list. "Is tomorrow too soon?"

"Tomorrow is perfect. Nine o'clock sharp and we can go over everything you'll need to know."

"I'll see you then, Devon. Thank you again. So, so much." He walked me to the door with an amused grin, that didn't offend me in the least. I was happy to have this job, excited that I wouldn't have to start over at the bottom of the ladder. At forty. I practically skipped back to my car with a grin so wide it made my face hurt, and the best part of all? The smile didn't leave for the rest of the day.

For the first time in two months, I could relax. I could breathe again and it wasn't all due to the dewy Tennessee air.

Preview: Midlife Do Over

* * *

Find out what happens when Pippa & Ryan inevitably run into each other in Midlife Do Over.
Scan the QR code:

Also by Piper Sullivan

Nanny Series

Curvy Nanny for the Nerd

Curvy Fake Wife for the Player

Curvy Nanny for the Grumpy Single Dad

Small Town Lovers

Midlife Baby: Morgot & Grady

Midlife Fake Out: Bella & Derek

Midlife Love Affair: Lacy & Levi

Midlife Valentine: Valona & Trey

Midlife Do Over: Pippa & Ryan

Healing Love

Dueling Drs, Book 6: Zola & Drew

Rockstar Baby Daddy, Book 5: Susie & Gavin

Unfriending the Dr, Book 4: Persy & Ryan

Kissing the Dr, Book 3: Megan & Casey

Loving the Nurse, Book 2: Gus & Antonio

Falling for the Dr, Book 1: Teddy & Cal

Curvy Girl Dating Agency

Forever Curves, Book 8: Brenna & Grant

Small Town Curves, Book 7: Shannon & Miles

Curvy Valentine Match, Book 6: Mara & Xander

Misbehaving Curves, Book 5: Joss & Ben

Curves for the Single Dad, Book 4: Tara & Chris

His Curvy Best Friend, Book 3: Sophie & Stone

Curvy Girl's Secret, Book 2: Olive & Liam

His Curvy Enemy, Book 1: Eva & Oliver

Small Town Protectors (Tulip Series)

That Hot Night, Book 12: Janey & Rafe

To Catch A Player, Book 11: Reece & Jackson

Cold Hearted Love, Book 10: Ginger & Tyson

Hero Boss, Book 9: Stevie & Scott

Dr's Orders, Book 8: Maxine & Derek

Mastering Her Curves, Book 7: Mikki & Nate

Kissing My Best Friend, Book 6: Bo & Jase

Undesired, Book 5: Hope & Will

Wanting Ms Wrong, Book 4: Audrey & Walker

Loving My Enemy, Book 3: Elka & Antonio

Bad Boy Benefits, Book 2: Penny & Ry

Hero In My Bed, Book 1: Nina & Preston

Accidental Hookups

Accidentally Hitched, Book 1: Viviana & Nash

Accidentally Wed, Book 2: Maddie & Zeke

Accidentally Bound, Book 3: Trish & Mason

Accidentally Wifed, Book 4: Magenta & Davis

Boardroom Games

His Takeover: An Enemies to Lovers Romance (Boardroom Games Book 1)

Sinful Takeover: An Enemies to Lovers Romance (Boardroom Games Book 2)

Naughty Takeover: An Enemies to Lovers Romance (Boardroom Games 3)

Boxsets & Collections

Small Town Misters: A Small Town Protectors Boxset

Misters of Pleasure: A Small Town Protectors Boxset

Misters of Love: A Small Town Romance Boxset

Misters of Passion: A Small Town Romance Boxset

Kiss Me, Love Me: An Alpha Male Romance Boxset

Accidentally On Purpose: A Marriage Mistake Boxset

Daddies & Nannies: A Contemporary Romance Boxset

Cowboys & Bosses: A Contemporary Romance Boxset

About the Author

Piper Sullivan is an old school romantic who enjoys reading romantic stories as much as she enjoys writing them.

She spends her time day-dreaming of dashing heroes and the feisty women they love.

Visit Piper's website www.pipersullivan.com

Join Piper's Newsletter for quirky commentary, new romance releases, freebies and contests.

Check her out on BookBub

Stalk her on Facebook

Printed in Dunstable, United Kingdom

78307175R00170